The Bridges in London

Michele Sobel Spirn

Learning Leaders

352 Park Avenue South • 13th Floor
New York NY 10010-1709

FOUR CORNERS PUBLISHING CO.

NEW YORK

Four Corners Publishing Company
45 West 10th Street, Suite 4J, New York, NY 10011

Printed in U.S.A.

Cover illustration by Catherine Huerta
Maps by Compass Projections, Anita Karl and Jim Kemp

03 04 02 01 00   5 4 3 2 1

Library of Congress Cataloging-in-Publication Data

Spirn, Michele.
        The Bridges of London / Michele Sobel Spirn. -- 1st ed.
        p. cm. -- (Going To)
        ISBN: 1-893577-00-7
        SUMMARY: There are plenty of mysteries to solve when
Robin and Joanna Bridge accompany their parents to London,
and the first one concerns a pen pal called Vivian. A short
guidebook to London is appended.
        1. London (England)--Juvenile fiction. 2. Pen pals--
Juvenile fiction. 3. London (England)--Guidebooks. I. Title.

PZ7.S757Bri 2000   [Fic]
                                          QBI99-846

For Steve and Josh,
my London companions,
and for Richard Hills,
thanks for the life.

CONTENTS

The Mystery of Vivian

 "Why are they taking so long?" asked Robin Bridge. Joanna, her younger sister, shifted from one foot to another in the long line snaking in front of the airline check-in counter.

"Don't ask me," she said. She looked at the guard who was standing near them, and smiled.

"They're looking for the Ripper," the guard said.

"Oh, that terrible killer, the one with the knives," said their mother. She pushed back her thick red hair, something she did whenever she was worried.

"Yes, he never goes anywhere without them," the guard said. "He's proud that no one's ever caught him with the knives."

"Let's hope he's not on this flight," said Mr. Bridge, dragging their heavy bags along. "It would be a shame if it were delayed or canceled."

"Don't even say something like that, Bob," said Mrs. Bridge. "We've looked forward to this trip to London for so long."

Soon the Bridges reached the front of the line. Mr. Bridge swung the bags onto the metal platform. Then he looked around at his daughters.

"Girls, you're going to have to check those bags," their mother said. "There just isn't that much room on the plane."

Robin really didn't mind. All she had in there was a few books. She had left the rest of the bag empty for the shopping she hoped to do. She took out a mystery book. Joanna grabbed some magazines from her own bag. Then they watched the matching gray cases glide away on the conveyor belt with the rest of their luggage.

On the plane, although it was late at night, Robin was too excited to sleep. She took out the letter she was carrying from her pen pal, Vivian.

15 June

Dear Robin,

Thanks for writing me for the pen pal project. I'm 14 and live in Alton, about an hour and a half by train from London. Does being in ninth grade mean that you're 14, too? What is Westbrook, New Jersey, like? What do you like to do? I like to go into London to visit my Uncle Peter. He owns a Japanese restaurant. He's jolly good fun. I'm glad you're coming to London. I'll meet you at your bed-and-breakfast. Cheers.

Vivian (Mountjoy)

Robin wondered about Vivian. She was curious about what her pen pal looked like. They had only exchanged one letter each. Robin's social studies teacher had assigned the project for the summer. In the fall, everybody would write reports about what they had learned from their pen pals. All of Robin's friends were envious that she would actually get to meet hers.

"You'll get an A for sure," they had said.

"Never mind that," Robin had replied. "I just hope she'll take me shopping. I heard they have all these cool stores in London, and I want to buy some British clothes." Robin had visions of coming back to school looking totally different, older, more sophisticated, less American, more British. She slid into a daydream…. Her red hair was piled on top of her head and she wore gobs of makeup. Everyone turned to stare at her. Her ears were pierced and she wore long, dangly green earrings. Just then, she heard a strange snorting sound. Her father was snoring. Her daydream shattered.

She looked at her mother and father dozing in the seats next to hers. Her father was going to Bath for a library conference almost as soon as they got to London. He'd be at the conference for a week and then would spend a few days with some old friends. But her mother would be around, doing research for her book on England in the 1600s. "I'll be lucky if she ever lets me out of the British Museum," Robin thought. "As for ear piercing, how often have I been told 'It's out of the question, Robin. No ear piercing, and that's final.'" Just then, as if echoing her thoughts, Joanna nudged her and said, "How are we going to escape once we get to London?"

"I'm thinking about it, Jo," said Robin. "Maybe Vivian can help. After all, if her parents let her go around London alone it must be safe."

Jo bounced up and down in her seat and clapped her hands.

"Was I ever that childish at twelve?" Robin wondered. Then she thought better of it. After all, the two of them were in this together.

"What do you think our hotel will be like?" she asked.

"I saw some pictures in a magazine the other day," Jo said

dreamily. "I think it will have pink flowered bedspreads, and a dressing table with pink frills, and a separate bathroom with a big tub and fluffy pink towels. They'll bring us breakfast in bed and pick up all our clothes."

"I don't know about that," Robin said. "But one good thing, we won't have to make our own beds."

Jo smiled. She hated making her bed.

"Let's plan to do some special things," she said.

"And no British Museum," Robin whispered.

"What's that?" her mother asked, sitting upright.

"Nothing, Mom," said Robin.

"Try and get some sleep, girls. We may be landing in London at nine-thirty in the morning British time, but it will really be the middle of the night by our time. I hope you won't be too tired. You can always take a nap when we get to the B&B."

"Tell us about the B&B," said Jo.

"You know that B&B is short for bed-and-breakfast, which is what you get. Your father and I stayed there on our honeymoon. It's called the St. Catherine, and it's in Russell Square, right near—"

"The British Museum," the two girls groaned.

"Never mind," said their father. "You girls could do with a little culture. Life isn't just shopping and reading magazines."

"I just hope the St. Catherine is the way we remember it," Mrs. Bridge said. "It was so romantic—a charming little room with a wash basin."

Alarms went off in Robin's head.

"Where's the bathroom?" she asked.

"They call it the loo in England," her father said. "It's down the hall. You'll be sharing it with other people in the B&B."

"How will I take a shower?" Robin asked. "I can't wear my bathrobe in the hall."

"I used to wear my raincoat as a bathrobe and take my clothes in with me."

Both Robin and Jo made faces at the idea, but their parents didn't see them. They had fallen asleep again. Soon the girls joined them.

They were wakened by the flight attendants coming around with hot towels, orange juice, and rolls. Then there were some customs forms that her father filled out for the family. Soon the plane was dipping low, flying over fields that were as green as Robin's birthstone ring. Robin's seat shook as the plane touched ground and rumbled down the runway. After they passed through Passport Control at Gatwick, they scrambled to get their luggage. Two other flights had come in at the same time. Bags were being tossed onto the carousel as fast as the crew could unload them.

"There!" Robin yelled and picked up her gray case. A minute later, Jo's case followed it. They pushed their bags past the green "Nothing to Declare" sign in the customs area.

"If you hurry, girls, we can make the next train to Victoria Station," their father said. He paid for the tickets. They ran down the platform, stumbling into a car just as the doors were closing. Looking out the window as the train pulled out of the station, they could see other travelers who hadn't made the train in time.

"Some of them look really upset," Robin said.

"Another train will come along soon, but I'm glad we didn't have to wait," said their mother. "It's a long enough ride as it is."

When they got to Victoria, Robin stared in amazement.

There was the longest escalator she had ever seen. It looked like a mountain to her.

"Now you see why they call it the Underground," her father said. "During World War II, people stayed here overnight during the bombing. Because some of these stations were so deep, they were the safest places in London."

As they rode up the escalator, Robin was bumped.

"Stand on the right," her father said.

When Robin moved over, she saw men and women race past her on the left. Then she noticed that there was a clear path on the left for those who wanted to run up the escalator. The people who stood on the right let the escalator carry them up. Bursts of song from men playing guitars followed them. As Robin looked back, she saw people throw coins in their guitar cases.

"They're called buskers," her mother said. "They're not supposed to beg in the tube station, but it's an old, old custom."

"The tube station?" asked Joanna.

"Just another way of saying 'the Underground,'" Mr. Bridge explained.

They rode on the Victoria line and changed at Green Park for the Piccadilly line to Russell Square. When they staggered out of the Underground, they saw a square filled with leafy, green trees, surrounded by small, white houses.

Mrs. Bridge pointed to one of them.

"There's our B&B."

They opened the iron gate and walked up the narrow, white stone steps. Inside, they waited in a small room with a television set and a couch covered in cracked brown leather until a woman came out to greet them.

"I'm Mrs. Bellaqua," she said, wiping her hands on her apron. Her black hair was pulled back in a tight bun.

"My husband and I stayed here a long time ago," Mrs. Bridge said. "I'm talking about seventeen years ago. You weren't the owner then, were you?"

"No," said the woman, "that was my father-in-law. We took it over when he passed on. My husband died eight years ago. Now it's just me."

"I'm sorry to hear that," said Mrs. Bridge. Behind her, the girls yawned.

"Keeping you awake, am I?" said Mrs. Bellaqua with a smile.

"Sorry. I'm just tired from the plane ride," Robin said.

"Then let's get you in your rooms." Mrs. Bellaqua went behind a counter and opened a notebook. Keys hung on hooks behind her. "Your name, luv?" she asked.

"We're the Bridges," said Mr. Bridge. Mrs. Bridge was busy looking around the room.

"It hasn't changed a bit," she said with a sigh.

"You're in Room Twenty and the girls are in Twenty-two," she said.

"Right near each other," Mrs. Bridge said.

"Well, that's a bit of a problem, that is. You see, there's a little staircase separating Twenty-two from Twenty. Room Twenty is really on the other side of the building. I'll show you," said Mrs. Bellaqua. She led them up a set of crooked, winding stairs and threw open the door to Room Twenty. The girls peeked in and saw a double bed, a chair, and a wash basin.

"Where is Room Twenty-two?" asked their father.

Mrs. Bellaqua showed them a tiny staircase. First, they went down. After five steps, they reached a landing.

"Now you turn over here and take the steps again," she said, climbing up another tiny staircase. "And here's your room."

Robin and Jo walked in and looked around. The room was very small. It was painted brown, not pink. There were two beds, but they were covered in dark green bedspreads. The same dark green material covered the windows. There wasn't a dressing table or a ruffle in sight.

"Will you girls be all right here on your own?"

"We're not babies, Mom," said Jo.

"We'll be fine," said Robin.

"After all, they're not that far away," their father said.

"Then it's settled?" asked Mrs. Bellaqua.

Mr. and Mrs. Bridge looked at each other. They both nodded.

"Yes," said Mrs. Bridge.

"I'll just show you the loo," Mrs. Bellaqua said.

The girls followed her into a small bathroom with a tub.

"Is there a shower?" Robin asked.

"Of course, luv," Mrs. Bellaqua said. She pointed to a metal contraption with a long cord that hung suspended from the wall.

Mrs. Bridge said, "I'll show you how to use it."

They clattered downstairs again. A tall, thin boy with shaggy brown hair and a torn green sweater was sitting on the couch.

"I'll be with you in a minute, luv," Mrs. Bellaqua said. She turned back to the Bridges and began telling them the hours for breakfast. Finally, they got their keys and were ready to haul their bags upstairs.

"Thank you, Mrs. Bellaqua," their father said.

"Ta, Mr. Bridge," she answered.

The boy on the couch got up. He looked at them as if they were strange animals from an unknown zoo.

"Excuse me," he said, "are you the Bridges from America?"

"Well, we're the London Bridges now," said Mr. Bridge.

The boy looked at Robin and Jo.

"Is one of you Robin?" he asked.

"I'm Robin."

The boy looked more surprised than ever.

"I thought you were a boy," he said.

"A boy," said Robin. "What do you mean?"

"Here, Robin is a boy's name. It's another name for Robert, what you call a nickname. Imagine that. I thought you were a boy all this time."

The idea seemed to tickle him, and he laughed.

Robin gave him her best snobby stare, the kind she used when someone played a joke on her or did something she didn't like.

"Excuse me, but who are you?"

The boy smiled and stuck out his hand.

"Hello, Robin. It's nice to meet you. I'm Vivian, Vivian Mountjoy, your pen pal."

CHAPTER TWO

The Mystery of the Missing Sushi Chef

 Robin couldn't help herself. She started laughing. Jo joined in.

"A boy! A boy!" they giggled.

Vivian smiled politely, but looked as if he didn't get the joke.

"All right, girls, that's enough," said Mrs. Bridge. "You see, Vivian, Robin may be a boy's name in England, but Vivian is a girl's name in the United States. That's why they're laughing."

"Oho," said Vivian, a real smile on his face now, "I should have realized. British names are so difficult."

"Do your friends call you Vivian?" Robin asked.

"Some do, but most call me after the initials of my first three names—Vivian Ian Charles. If it's more comfortable for you, why don't you call me Vic."

"Great," said Jo, "you sure don't look like a Vivian to me." She giggled again.

Mrs. Bridge frowned at her. "I'm sure Americans have names for other things that sound strange to you," she said. "I remember you have another name for trucks."

"Yes, we call them lorries," said Vivian.

"And what we call elevators, you call lifts," Mr. Bridge said.

"You have another name for biscuits, too, don't you?" asked Vivian.

"Yes," said Mrs. Bridge. "We call them cookies."

"What do you call pizza?" asked Jo, hoping for something really unusual.

"Pizza," said Vic, laughing.

"It's been nice to meet you, Vic," Mrs. Bridge said. "That long plane trip is really catching up with me. I need a nap. Come on, girls."

"I thought perhaps you might let the girls come with me while you nap," Vic said. "They could see a bit of London, and get accustomed to it."

"I don't know," said Mrs. Bridge, looking at Mr. Bridge. "We haven't been in London for a long time. Is it still as safe as it once was?"

"Absolutely," said Vic. "Of course, the girls will be safe with me. I thought I might take them to Chinatown. My uncle has a Japanese restaurant there."

"Is your uncle Japanese?" Robin asked.

"No, he's British. But Uncle Peter studied Japanese at university and fell in love with the country. He decided the best way to get to know more Japanese people was to open a restaurant."

"He sounds like an unusual man," said Mr. Bridge.

"Oh, it's been a wild success," Vic said. "Everyone loves the place. I'm sure the girls would like to see it."

"I don't know," said their mother. She looked at Mr. Bridge.

"Oh, please, please," said Jo. Robin felt she was too old to beg, but she held her breath nevertheless.

Then their parents nodded at each other.

"All right," Mrs. Bridge said, "but be back in a few hours. You can nap before we go to the Ceremony of the Keys at the Tower."

They ran out the door and down the steps before Mr. and Mrs. Bridge could say anything more.

"This is great!" said Jo. "We're free. We don't have to look at any boring museum exhibits yet. We can just walk down the street and look around."

"Well, I'm afraid we have to go on the Underground to get to Chinatown. But it's only three stops. Do you have your Travelcards?"

"No, what are those?" asked Robin.

"For a few pounds, you can travel all week on one pass."

He showed them how to take their photographs at the little booth in the tube station. They waited for a few minutes and the little black-and-white pictures slid out. Then a woman behind the ticket counter took their money and their pictures and gave each girl a card with her photograph on it.

"I feel like a real Londoner," said Robin as she waved her card at the guard and stepped onto the escalator. Soon both girls were busy staring at the ads that lined the platform, seeing pictures that showed products that were strange to them. Just as their mother had said, cookies were called biscuits, and there was a big picture of "ginger biscuits" on their left.

Then the train came gliding in.

"Did you notice that the train just slides into the station, it doesn't roar in like a New York subway?" Robin said.

She and Jo seated themselves on the seats covered in thick red plush, while Vic hung onto the bar above them.

A few stops later they ran upstairs and out into Leicester Square.

"Look!" cried Robin. She pointed to the newspaper headlines that were mounted for passersby to see.

In huge black letters they said: "DID YANKS LET RIPPER SLIP?"

"Like a paper, luv?" The newsman crouched by the side of his stand waited for her to decide.

Vic handed the man a few coins and Robin took the paper from the newsman's grimy hand.

"It says the Ripper might be here. That he might have come over to England. I wonder if he was on our plane," she said.

The man smiled at Robin. "Better watch out, luv, the Ripper likes pretty girls like you!"

Vic scowled at the man and moved the girls away from the stand.

"Come on," he said, "my uncle's restaurant is just a few streets away. But I'll show you Leicester Square first."

They walked past a few cafes and a pizza stand and came to a huge square. On all sides it was surrounded by buildings—mostly restaurants and movie theaters. In the middle was a pretty park, where people lay on the grass or picnicked or read newspapers on the benches.

"They like to take advantage of the sun when the weather is good," said Vic.

"Isn't it like this all the time during the summer?" asked Jo.

"I'm afraid not. Haven't you ever heard that joke: What's the shortest day of the year in Great Britain?"

"No, what's the answer?"

"The summer."

Robin looked ahead and saw a crowd of people.

"What's up there?" she asked.

Vic looked at his watch. "Oh, good, it's just noon. Let's go see."

They joined the crowd in time to see little figures march out from an ornate clock suspended above the Swiss Centre. On one side a little woman dressed in a red blouse and white apron moved in time to music coming from the clock. On the other, a small man in red and purple robes did the same. They finally stopped when the clock chimed the hour.

When the performance was over, Robin looked around. Musicians were playing near the park, people were strolling with ice cream cones, and a few boys skated through on in-line skates.

"It's so full of life. I never thought London would be like this," she said.

They walked back through the square and Vic steered them through a tiny alley and into a long, curved street. All of a sudden the scene changed. Now they were passing cramped stores and small restaurants with signs written in Chinese. Chinese men hauled crates of green vegetables through restaurant doors. Passing a courtyard, Jo and Robin saw a young boy peeling carrots.

"Mmm! Smells good," said Jo, sniffing the savory cooking smell of fried garlic.

"I took you the back way," said Vic. "It's a short cut. The main part of Chinatown is much more impressive. You enter through a big red wooden gate. Next time, I'll take you that way."

Robin and Jo were entranced with the streets, which were paved with cobblestones.

"It looks so old," Jo said.

"Everything in London is old," said Vic. "The city has been here for over two thousand years."

"There were British here two thousand years ago?" asked Robin.

"Actually, it was built by the Romans. You can still see some of the Roman walls in the Museum of London."

"Not another museum," said Jo. "I'll pass."

"Never mind," said Vic. "Here's my uncle's restaurant."

Robin looked up to see a wooden building hung with white Japanese lanterns. A small red sign said: Edo.

Vic slid a door open and wiped his feet on a mat. He motioned the girls inside. A small room was decorated with pictures of Japan. Diners sat at wooden tables and on stools at the sushi bar. The room was steamy and smelled like bean soup and steak.

Behind a counter, adding up totals on a computer, was a tall, blond man who looked up when they came in.

"Hello, Vic," he said.

"Hi, Uncle Peter. These are my friends from America, Robin and Joanna."

The tall blond man got up and shook their hands.

"Can I offer you something to drink?" he asked.

A Japanese waitress with short black hair brought them cold soft drinks.

Uncle Peter sat down with them but kept glancing anxiously at the door.

"What's the matter, Uncle?" asked Vic.

"My new sushi chef hasn't turned up, and he was supposed to be here by now. I'm worried about him. He doesn't speak much English, and I'm afraid he's gotten lost."

"He has your phone number, doesn't he?" Vic asked.

"Yes, that's true," Uncle Peter said. "He'll turn up, I'm sure."

"What's sushi?" asked Jo.

"It's raw fish and rice," Uncle Peter said.

Jo couldn't help making a face.

"I bet if you tried it you'd like it," Uncle Peter said.

"Never in a million years," Jo said.

He changed the subject.

"What are you planning to see in London?"

"Anything but the British Museum," Jo said.

"You should take them to Covent Garden," he said to Vic.

"That is a lot of fun," Vic said. "We could go now. It's not that far from here."

Robin drained the last drop from her soft drink and said, "I'm ready."

As they said good-bye to Uncle Peter, he said, "Come back for dinner tomorrow night and bring your parents. I'd like to meet them."

"Will I have to eat raw fish?" Jo asked.

"I'll have a plate of it made especially for you," Uncle Peter teased. He looked at his watch and became serious.

"None of us will be eating sushi if my chef doesn't turn up."

Jo was still wrinkling her nose as Vic led the girls away.

"Don't worry," he said. "Uncle Peter has lots of cooked food on the menu too."

"Will we need our Travelcards to get to Covent Garden?" Robin asked.

"No, we can walk from here," said Vic. "You know, Covent

Garden was once the main market in London for fruits and vegetables. Then the fruit and vegetable market moved, and the whole area became filled with shops and restaurants."

They walked through a narrow alley filled with shops and crossed the street.

"Remember, look left," Vic said. "You drive on the other side of the road from us."

"I can't believe how crowded it is here," Robin said.

"It's the season for visitors," Vic said, "plus lots of people come here to study."

Robin and Jo kept looking around as they walked. Some people were lunching at a sidewalk cafe. A sign announced: "Cream Teas." They passed tiny old-fashioned shops filled with woolen sweaters and scarves and then a big, modern supermarket.

"It's the same and it's different," Robin said. "Some of this looks like home, but just when I think it's all the same, something reminds me that we're not home, we're in London."

"And here we are," said Vic. "Covent Garden."

Robin had imagined that Covent Garden would be like its name, filled with flowers and green plants. Instead, she saw a tall, gray, stone building surrounded by cobblestone streets.

"Look! A puppet show!" cried Jo. She rushed over to join the crowd of children and adults who were being entertained by Punch and Judy. The three of them watched for a while, then were lured away by a juggler tossing flaming batons. Finally, they ended up listening to a woman who sang and played guitar.

"It's a lot more than just shops and restaurants," Robin said.

"It sure is," said Jo. "It's great. But there's just one problem."

"What's that?" asked Vic.

"I'm starving."

"That's easy," said Vic. He took them to the middle of the gray building where they walked down some steps. All around them were little stalls where people were selling silver, china, and jewelry. Robin wanted to stop at the jewelry stall but Jo pulled her along.

They sat down at a table outside and Vic got them sandwiches and drinks. As they ate and talked, Robin was horrified to find herself yawning. Then Jo started yawning.

"You must be tired," Vic said politely.

"It's just that we never slept on the plane," said Robin. "We were so excited about coming here."

"Why don't I take you back to your B&B, and then we can make some plans for tomorrow?"

Robin smiled. "I'd love to do that."

As they walked back on the cobblestone street, Robin kept glancing over her shoulder.

"What are you looking at?" Jo asked.

"I've got the creepiest feeling," Robin said. "I feel as if someone's watching me."

Jo looked at the crowd of people around them.

"I don't see anything," she said.

"I must be imagining it," said Robin. But as they walked down the steps to the Underground, she thought she caught someone staring at her.

Then Jo pulled at her and yelled, "Come on, slowpoke, Vic's waiting."

CHAPTER THREE

The Mystery of the Shower

"We should unpack," said Robin, jumping up from her bed after her nap.

"I still feel sleepy," Jo said, stretching and yawning. "Let's leave it for later."

"Okay," said Robin. "I think I'll take a shower."

Remembering her father's advice, she wrapped herself in her raincoat, and stepped into her sneakers without bothering to put them all the way on. She shuffled down the hall to the bathroom.

Once inside, she stared at the strange hanging shower. She pushed it and it swayed to and fro. Then she bent down and turned the water on, but nothing came from the shower.

"I don't want a bath," she said to herself. "I'll figure out this shower if I have to stay here all afternoon."

She pushed a knob. Nothing happened. She pulled a lever and, all of a sudden, water squirted into her face, then all over the tiny bathroom.

"Agh!" yelled Robin. She wiped her face on the sleeve of her raincoat. Then she grabbed the shower. Wrestling with it, Robin freed it from its hook. The shower fell into the tub, spraying water all over the tiled walls.

Frantically, Robin grabbed the faucets. She turned them and, magically, the shower stopped spraying. Now only a little trickle of water ran out.

"I'm soaking wet, and I haven't even washed up yet," Robin thought. She looked around for a towel, then snapped her fingers.

"Of course, I have to get one from the room."

Back she scuffed down the hall.

"How was the shower?" asked Jo. "I'm thinking of taking one myself."

"Don't ask," said Robin. "I haven't taken one yet."

"But you're all wet!"

"I said, don't ask!"

She grabbed a towel and went back to the bathroom. The door was closed.

"I thought I left it open," Robin said. She turned the handle but the door was locked.

"Occupado!" someone called.

Robin waited in the hall, dripping on the brown linoleum that covered the floor. Finally, a young, dark-haired man in a T-shirt and jeans came out and flashed a smile at Robin.

This time, Robin made sure the shower was fastened. She took off her raincoat, and got ready to step into the tub.

"Oh, no!" she cried. She had forgotten her soap and her shampoo.

"What happened now?" asked Jo, when Robin came into the room. Robin scowled and muttered something. She grabbed her shower things and ran back to the bathroom. She was just in time to see the bathroom door close. Robin waited patiently for whoever was in there to come out. Five minutes passed, then ten.

"There must be another bathroom around here," she thought.

Finally, when she was just about to give up, a blonde woman came out.

"Oh, sorry," she said, "I didn't know anyone was waiting. I usually have the lav all to meself at this time of day. Next time, just knock, luv."

Robin ran into the bathroom. She locked the door. She took off her raincoat and climbed into the tub. She turned on the shower.

It was great. Warm water ran over her. She soaped herself and then her hair.

"Eek!"

The warm water had changed to freezing cold without any warning. Robin fiddled with the faucets but the icy water continued to pour down on her. She had no choice. Gritting her teeth, she endured the cold water until all the soap was out of her hair. Then she jumped out of the tub, shivering and shaking.

Back in the room, she told Jo all about her shower adventures.

"I think I'll skip my shower," Jo said.

"At least the cold water woke me up. I'm not sleepy any more."

Robin rubbed her short hair dry and pulled on a clean pair of jeans and a white shirt.

"Let's wake Mom and Dad," she said. "I'm starved."

The girls clattered down the staircase, crossed the landing, and climbed up the stairs to their parents' room.

"Knock, knock," yelled Jo.

"Who's there?" asked their mother.

"The London Bridges," answered Jo.

"The London Bridges who?" responded her father.

"The London Bridges who are falling down from hunger," said Jo.

Their father opened the door.

"Enter, miladies."

The girls found their mother on the bed looking at a guidebook.

"We were just trying to find a place to eat before we go to the ceremony," she said. "Which would you like—Chinese food or Indian?"

"What's Indian food like?" asked Robin.

"Spicy and delicious," said their father. "I vote for Indian."

"If we don't like it, can we get pizza later?" Jo asked.

"I'm sure you'll like it," said their mother.

"Indian food tonight, Japanese food tomorrow night," Jo grumbled, "we sure are eating some strange things. And if Vic's uncle makes me eat raw fish, I'm definitely going to throw up."

"Vic told you his uncle has other things on the menu," Robin said.

"Yeah, probably fried porcupine and boiled worms," Jo said.

"You're such a baby," Robin said. "You never want to try anything new."

"I'm not a baby. Just because I like plain food..."

"Girls, let's go," Mr. Bridge said. "I didn't bring you to London to bicker. Robin, stop teasing your sister. Jo, you'll try Indian food tonight. I'm sure there'll be chances in the future to get pizza."

As they walked to the restaurant their parents had chosen, the girls passed many other restaurants, most of them Indian.

"Why are there so many Indian restaurants here?" Robin asked.

"That's because India was once ruled by Great Britain. Many people from India came here, just as some British settled in India."

They stopped in front of a small yellow building with a green sign that said: Star of India.

"Here we are," their father said.

They were in a dark room filled with tables covered with white cloths. Only a few people were in the restaurant.

"Nobody's here," Jo said.

"That's because we're eating unusually early," her mother said. "Most people in London eat later than 6:30 p.m. But we want to be on time for the Ceremony of the Keys. And we still have to get to the Tower of London."

A waiter in a dark green jacket hurried over to them, seated them, and handed them menus.

"What's tandoori, Dad?" Robin asked.

"It's food baked in a special hot oven. Try the tandoori chicken. I think you'll like it."

When their food came, Jo bit into a piece of puffy Indian bread.

"Mmm! Good. If it had some tomato sauce on it, it would taste like pizza."

"I like the tandoori chicken," Robin said. "It's spicy but not too hot."

By the time they had finished their meal, Jo admitted she liked the Indian food.

"I just wish we were eating this tomorrow night," she said.

"Maybe you'll be surprised. You were surprised you liked this tonight, weren't you?"

"Let's go," said Mr. Bridge. "We still have to take two trains to get to the Tower. We can't be even one minute late. One time I went and reached the gate at one minute past nine."

"What happened?" Robin asked.

"They wouldn't let me in. They said the ceremony always started on time with no exceptions. I begged and said I had come all the way from America to see it, but they simply said no."

"Poor Dad," Robin said. "We'll be really early this time."

At the station, Mrs. Bridge pointed out the electric signs overhead.

"Kennington. Three minutes. What does that mean?" asked Jo.

"It means that the train's last stop is Kennington, and it'll be in this station in three minutes."

"Cool," said Robin. "You never have to guess when your train's coming."

By the time they got to the Tower stop, Jo's head was drooping.

"I don't know why I'm so tired," she said.

"It's jet lag," said Mrs. Bridge. "Because of the time difference here, your body hasn't caught up. In a few days, you'll be okay."

They walked to a tall, black, iron gate. A man in a police uniform checked their tickets and let them in.

They walked across the cobblestones and joined a small group of people waiting in the growing darkness. In the distance they heard a clock strike. Bong, bong—it chimed nine times.

"That's right, ladies and gentlemen. Nine o'clock and all's well here at the Tower," said a man dressed in a black and red uniform. A red crown was embroidered on the front of his jacket, with big red letters "ER" underneath.

"Welcome to the Ceremony of the Keys. This ceremony has been going on uninterrupted for seven hundred years. I know I don't look that old, but looks are deceiving," he joked. "In a few minutes, what you'll see is the changing of the Tower guard. One group of guardsmen will hand over the keys to another group. But before they do, I'd like to point out a few sights here."

He led them over to a small stone building with a gate in its arch. Looking through it, Robin and Jo could see water.

"This is the famous Traitors' Gate. You'd come up here by boat hundreds of years ago. And if they took you up the Thames River and in this way, you knew you probably wouldn't come out alive. Maybe you'd done something to offend the king or queen, maybe you'd tried to take over the throne—it had to be something pretty big—but they'd bring you here and lock you up in the Tower until they got the order to chop off your head."

He fell silent for a minute, and they could hear the splashing of the water. Robin shivered, imagining the men rowing her up to the gate and dragging her up to the Tower.

"I'd like to tell you more about some of the pleasant things that happened here. There's a block over there where Anne Boleyn's head was cut off and we've got some other cheery sites, too, but it's time for the ceremony, ladies and gentlemen, so I'll ask you to keep quiet now."

Robin looked around. It had gotten darker now and the mist was rising from the River Thames. The air was foggy and she wasn't sure of the shapes in the distance. Were they men or ghosts?

The thud of feet on the cobblestones reassured her. Men dressed like the guardsman marched forward towards another group of men. Commands were given. Then one guardsman handed the keys over to another and each group marched off.

As the marching sounds faded away, their guide said, "Now that may not look like much, but to us it means all's right in our world. The ceremony is held, the tradition goes on, and our nation is preserved. We've got a lot of customs like that. You'll have to come back in the day to see them, but we've got a flock of ravens living here. Ravens aren't particularly pretty. They make a lot of noise. Most people would run them off. But not us. Why? Because there's a legend that says that if the ravens ever leave the Tower, it will crumble and England will fall. So, ladies and gentlemen, we've got those blinking birds on the payroll forever."

Robin looked up. It was getting foggier and darker. She could hear the sound of foghorns coming from the river.

"Now I'll give you a few minutes and then I'll have to see you out. Take a quick look round. The Tower is a special place at night."

Jo and her parents walked back towards Traitors' Gate. But Robin decided to go the other way. She sensed other people in the fog. She couldn't see them until she was almost on top of them.

"This fog is becoming a real pea souper," she heard a woman say.

"Very British," a man responded.

Robin passed them. Now she was all alone. The silence was eerie. It was dark.

"What a place for a mystery," Robin thought.

Click! Click! She heard footsteps behind her. Her sneakers made no sound on the cobblestones. Who was it?

"Mom? Is that you?"

There was no answer. Robin walked faster. Click! Click! Click! The person behind her walked faster, too.

"Dad?"

No answer. This was becoming too much like some of Robin's favorite mystery books. Her heart started thudding. She wasn't sure what to do. If she turned around and ran back to her parents and Jo, she would be running straight towards the person following her.

Robin froze. Maybe if she stayed absolutely still, the person would pass her by. She tried to hold her breath. Click! Click! The person was coming closer.

She could feel the breeze from someone coming nearer. She heard someone grunt. Then she felt a hand on her shoulder.

"Eek!" Robin shrieked and ran. As she raced away, she heard something that sounded like "sorry," but she didn't stop to hear anymore. Even if the person had made a mistake, it seemed as if he had tried to scare her.

"Help! Help!" she screamed. Her father caught her as she ran into him.

"Robin! What's the matter!"

"Someone was following me!" she panted. "I got away." She started to cry.

Her father hugged her.

"You're all right now. I'll find him." He started to walk away, but Robin grabbed him.

"No, don't leave. Please."

By the time Jo and Mrs. Bridge joined them, Robin had calmed down and Mr. Bridge had told the guard what had happened.

"Probably a mistake," he said. "This fog is thick tonight. Maybe someone wanted to play a joke on the young lady. At any rate, she's all right, and it's time to go."

He ushered them out the gate. Jo and Mrs. Bridge went ahead. Robin and her father walked behind. As Robin looked back at the gate, she saw the guard open it again and a thin shadow slipped out into the fog.

CHAPTER FOUR

The Mystery of the Knives

 "Whew! I'm tired," said Jo, flopping onto the bed. "I'm wide awake now," Robin said. "I think I'll unpack."

"Fine," said Jo. "Just don't make too much noise. I'm going to sleep." She rummaged in her bag and found a pair of pajamas. She changed quickly and slipped into bed. Soon she was snoring.

Robin tackled her big bag first and put away her clothes. When that was empty, she picked up her gray case. She put it on the bed and tried to undo the catch. The case didn't fly open the way it usually did.

"I could leave it until the morning," she thought, "but I really want to finish reading my mystery." It was about a girl who discovered a treasure map and how she outwitted the thieves who were following her.

Robin tried her case again. Again the catches resisted her pressure. Finally, she banged on it with her fist and pressed against the catches with all of her might.

"Whoa!" The case flew open. Instead of mystery books and odds and ends, there lay an array of sharp, glistening knives.

Robin took a few steps back from the case. She had never seen so many knives together in her life. Each one looked sharper than the next. Irresistibly, they drew her forward. She leaned over and touched one. "Ouch!" She almost cut herself.

Where was her case? How did she get the knives? Whose were they? Who traveled with knives like these? The only person she could think of was...

"Jo! Jo! Wake up!" She shook her sister's shoulder hard.

"Mmmphnmx?" Jo snuggled deeper into her pillow.

"Jo! I need you. Wake up now!"

Jo put the pillow over her head to drown out the sound of Robin's voice.

"Jo, it's an emergency!"

"Wha? Wha?" Jo poked her head out from under the pillow and looked up with bleary eyes.

"Come see what I found."

"I don't care. I told you not to wake me up. I'm trying to get over that jet sag or lag or whatever Mom called it. I'm too tired to see anything."

Robin picked up the case and stuck it under Jo's nose.

"Knives! What are you doing with those, Robin Bridge? They're sharp and dangerous. Where did you get them from?"

"That's what I'm trying to figure out," Robin said.

"Put those away right now!" Jo sat up in bed, her eyes open wide.

Robin closed the case and put it under her bed.

"That looks just like your case," Jo said. "Where is yours?"

"That's just it," said Robin. "I started to unpack it, thinking it was mine. Instead, I found those knives."

Jo jumped off the bed and ran to get her case.

"Whew! That's a relief. Mine is okay," she said. "I thought I might find it stuffed with guns."

"So only mine is missing," Robin said. "That means that there was a mix-up in the airport. That's the only place it could have happened."

"You don't think somebody could have taken your case on the train, or in the Underground, or even traded it for his or hers in our room?"

"Why would they do that?" Robin asked.

"Maybe to get rid of the knives temporarily," Jo said. She glanced over at the newspaper they had gotten.

"Of course!" Robin screamed. "They're the Ripper's. He was afraid the police might be looking for a man carrying a case full of knives. So he switched cases with me."

"He was lucky our cases look just like his," Jo said.

"There are millions of cases that look like ours. I'm just surprised there weren't any others on our flight."

"Do you think he knows you have the knives?"

Robin shuddered. "He must. I bet he'll be coming back for them."

She went over and checked the lock on their door. Then she pushed a chair up against it.

"I don't think he'll break in," said Robin. "That would make too much of a fuss. I think he'll find another way."

"First, let's hide the case," Jo said.

They looked for a good place.

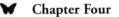

"There aren't too many hiding places here," Jo said. "There's so little furniture."

"I just remembered something. I read it in one of my mysteries," Robin said. She pushed the green curtains away from the window. There was a ledge inside big enough to rest the case on. She put it there and covered it up with the curtain again.

"Perfect," Jo said. She climbed into bed again.

"How can you sleep?" Robin asked.

"Easily. We've locked the door, and the chair is jammed up against it. You yourself said the Ripper won't break into the room, it would make too much of a fuss. So I'm going to sleep, and I'll think more about it in the morning."

Soon her sister was snoring from the next bed. But Robin tossed and turned. She was used to reading herself to sleep. She tried one of Jo's magazines, but it wasn't as gripping as the mystery she was reading.

Jo turned over and stopped snoring and the room was quiet. Soon Robin felt her head nodding over an article titled "20 Ways to Reshape Your Eyebrows." While she was asleep, she kept dreaming the Ripper was raising his eyebrows at her, saying, "Let me help you. I'll just get my knives."

She was running from him, and she had almost gotten away when she heard the pounding of his footsteps. Thud, thud, thud.

"No! No! Please help me!" she cried. She woke with a start, her heart thudding.

"Robin! Jo! Time to get up!"

It was their father, knocking to wake them up.

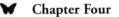

"What do you want, Dad?"

"Hurry up and get dressed. Otherwise you'll miss breakfast."

Robin shook Jo awake, and they both washed up and got dressed quickly.

"Did I dream about it or was that a case of knives we found last night?" Jo asked.

Robin flipped the curtains back.

"No, we certainly didn't dream about it," she said. "Let's eat breakfast first, and then we'll come back up and talk about what to do. I'm beginning to have some ideas."

The girls walked down the stairs and into a crowded breakfast room. In one corner, an Indian man with a beard and a turban sat eating toast. Near him, two African students in dashikis were reading the newspaper and drinking tea. Some Japanese men and women were talking at a center table. And in the far corner, their parents were seated at a table for four, waving at them.

"Just in time," said their father.

Mrs. Bellaqua came over to them, smoothing back her hair.

"How would you like your eggs, luv?"

"Sunny side up," Robin said.

"Scrambled," said Jo.

"Chocolate to drink all right?"

"Fine," both girls said.

Mrs. Bridge poured tea from a big brown teapot for herself and Mr. Bridge.

"How did you girls sleep?"

"Fine, but somebody woke me up to tell me—Ouch!"

"What's the matter, Jo?" their father asked.

"Nothing," said Robin, glaring at her.

Just then Mrs. Bellaqua slid plates in front of them.

"Now that's hot, so be careful."

Robin looked at her plate.

"This is just like the English breakfast they're always talking about in mysteries," she said.

Two sunny-side up eggs were ringed by sausages and fried tomatoes. Something black lay near the tomatoes.

"What's that?" asked Jo, poking it with her fork.

"A fried mushroom," said her father, taking a bite out of his. "Mmm, delicious!"

Mrs. Bellaqua placed a rack of toast on the table.

"There's butter and marmalade in the dish here. And I'll be back in a tick with your chocolate."

For a few minutes everyone ate heartily without speaking.

"I was really hungry," Mrs. Bridge said. "Must be the time difference."

"I don't think so," said Mr. Bridge. "It's three a.m. back home in New Jersey. I don't think we're accustomed to eating meals then. I think you're hungry just because you see other people eating breakfast."

"Always the professor," Mrs. Bridge said, laughing.

"That reminds me. This professor better start making plans to get to his conference in Bath," Mr. Bridge said.

"What time do you leave, Dad?" Robin asked.

"My train leaves at ten a.m.," he said.

"We're going to miss you," Jo said. "Do you have to go?"

"That's part of the reason for this trip," he said. "But I'll be back in a few days. Then we'll do something special. In the meantime, I leave you in good hands—with your mother."

"Thanks for that vote of confidence," Mrs. Bridge said. "Don't worry, girls. We'll have a good time. But you will have to abide by my rules. We're in a strange city, and we have to be careful."

"I'll say," muttered Jo. Robin dug her with her elbow.

"Help me get my bags ready," Mr. Bridge said to his wife.

They walked upstairs and the girls went to their own room.

"What did you kick me for?" said Jo, as soon as they had shut the door.

"You almost gave away everything," Robin said. "You and your big mouth. Remember how great it was to go out with Vic yesterday, and how free we were? Do you think Mom would let us go out on our own if she knew about the knives?"

"I guess not," Jo said.

"I know she wouldn't," Robin said. "Even the idea of Dad leaving made her talk about rules and listening to her. She'd go berserk if she found out about the knives."

"What are we going to do?" asked Jo.

"I've got some ideas," Robin said. "I've learned a lot from reading mysteries."

"Like what?"

"In the first place, we can set traps for the Ripper. We can find out if anyone comes near the room, and tries to steal the case."

"How can we do that?"

"Give me some of your hair."

"What?"

"You heard me. Pull out a few of your hairs."

"No. You pull out one of yours."

"I can't. Mine are too short. You have longer hair."

With a sigh and a small shriek, Jo pulled out a few hairs.

"Here. What are you going to do with them?"

"We're going to put them on the door handle when we go out," Robin said. "If the hair isn't there when we come back, then we know someone came in."

"Okay," said Jo. "That's good. That'll give us a warning if the Ripper is around."

"And we'll do something else," Robin said. She took a small can of bath powder from the top of the dresser. She sprinkled the powder on the floor near the curtains.

"Aha! So if the Ripper goes near the curtains, we'll see his footprints in the powder," Jo said.

"Exactly," said Robin.

"There's just one thing you've forgotten, my dear Sherlock," Jo said. "What are we going to do with the Ripper if we catch him?"

"Girls!" their mother called. "Let's go. Your father's ready to leave."

"I haven't figured that out yet," Robin said. "But give me time."

"I just hope the Ripper will. Give you time, that is."

CHAPTER FIVE

The Mystery of the Disappearing Powder

 "Good-bye, Dad! Have a great time!" Robin and Jo waved from the door of St. Catherine's as their father got into a big, black taxicab.

Their mother came up the steps after kissing her husband good-bye. She smiled at the girls.

"We'll miss Dad, but I've got something special planned today."

"What's that?" asked Jo.

"It's a mystery. Get your things, and I'll wait for you here."

"A mystery. I know I'll like it," Robin said.

The day was cool and gray, even though it was July. Robin and Jo grabbed sweaters and umbrellas. As they scrambled down the steps, they heard the high whine of a vacuum cleaner in the background. Mrs. Bellaqua and a woman with a blue scarf wrapped around her head were vacuuming the carpet.

Outside, their mother led them to the Holborn stop on the Underground and they took the train one stop to Oxford Circus.

"Is this the surprise? Are we going to the circus?" Jo asked.

"No, it's not that kind of circus," their mother said. "In England, a circus is an open square or a circle where several streets come together."

"Like Piccadilly Circus," Robin said.

Jo looked sulky. "I wish we were going to a real circus."

"Never mind. I think you'll like what I've planned."

They changed trains and ended up at Baker Street. Robin looked at the street sign.

"I think I'm beginning to guess where we're going," she said.

"Where? Tell me," Jo begged.

"You'll see," said Robin.

They walked down a long block of brown stone buildings and stopped outside one of them, where a group was gathered around a guide. She waited until the Bridges joined the group.

"Welcome to 221B Baker Street, where the famous Sherlock Holmes and his friend, Dr. Watson, lived. Of course, as everyone knows, Sherlock Holmes, the detective, really only lived in the mind of Sir Arthur Conan Doyle who brought him to life in 1887 with *Study in Scarlet.* Yet, for millions of people around the world, Sherlock Holmes is so real they were disappointed to learn that no 221B Baker Street ever existed. That's why we opened the Sherlock Holmes Museum."

"I might have known why you guessed," muttered Jo. "It had to be something with mysteries and detectives."

The guide escorted them into the house and asked them to wait at the first room they came to.

"As fans of the great detective know, he rented rooms in this house from Mrs. Hudson, who never seemed to have a clue about how her famous lodger actually solved his cases. In these rooms, you'll see a faithful recreation of how Holmes might have lived, based on clues from the stories. Please take time to look around, and mind the stairs—they are narrow."

Robin wandered, as if in a dream, gazing at the famous dressing gown draped over a chair and looking into the cozy gas fire that was lit in every room.

"Imagine, they've even put in his butterfly collection," Robin said to her mother.

"It's a wonderful look at what a nineteenth-century London home looked like," she said.

Jo was less enthusiastic. "How long do we have to stay here?"

"I guess it means a lot less if you haven't read the stories," her mother said.

"I'll loan you one when we get back home," Robin said. "I really think you'd like *The League of Red-Headed Men.*"

She started to tell Jo the story as they walked around the rooms.

"And then what happened?" Jo asked.

"I think you've gotten interested in Sherlock," her mother said. "But I'm getting more interested in lunch. I see they have a restaurant next door."

When the hostess seated them in the Victorian dining room, Jo and Robin looked at the menu eagerly.

"Bubble and squeak! What's that?" Robin asked.

"And Welsh Rarebit! I know I've never had that," Jo said.

"I wouldn't bet on that, dearie," their waitress said. "It's just hot cheese and toast."

"Like a grilled cheese sandwich?" Robin asked.

"A bit like it. Bubble and squeak now—I'm not sure you'd like that," she said. "It's mostly fried cabbage."

"Ugh! I'll have the Welsh Rarebit," said Jo.

"Me, too," said Robin.

"You can make it three," said their mother. "I'm not that fond of cabbage. I'm off to find the loo."

"We'll wait here," Robin said.

They watched their mother walk towards the back of the restaurant.

"Did you get any good ideas?" Jo asked.

"What do you mean?"

"About trapping the Ripper. You must have picked up something from all that Sherlock Holmes stuff," Jo said.

"I actually forgot to think about it," Robin said. "But, don't worry, I'll come up with something."

"Here we are," said the waitress, placing three hot plates on the table.

"This is good," said Jo. She took another bite of hot cheese.

"If nothing else, this trip has certainly gotten you to eat other things besides pizza," their mother said, sliding into her chair.

"Where are we going next?" Jo asked.

"There are two possibilities," their mother said. "We could go to Madame Tussaud's or—"

"Let's go to Madame Tussaud's. I'd really love to see all the waxworks of famous people," Jo said.

"How do you know about that?" asked Mrs. Bridge.

"It tells about it in my guidebook," Jo said.

As they walked to Marylebone Road, Jo entertained them by reading out the names of famous people whose likenesses were modeled in wax and placed in the museum:

"Napoleon, Marilyn Monroe, Eddie Murphy, Henry VIII and his six wives, John F. Kennedy, Richard the Lionhearted..."

She was still talking as they walked up the steps to the museum. Once inside, they stopped to ask directions from a small bald man standing next to the coatroom.

"Excuse me, which way—Oh, for goodness' sake..." Mrs. Bridge and the girls started laughing. The man was a wax statue.

"He looked really real," Robin said. "I was about to talk to him myself."

"That's the best statue we have, Madame," said one of the guards. "Many people are fooled every day. In fact, they've been fooled for nearly two hundred years."

"Is that when Madame Tussaud started the museum?" Robin asked.

"Yes, she brought it over from France in 1802, and we've been going strong ever since."

"You mean the same statues have been here since then?" asked Jo.

"No, we change statues quite a bit—except for the historical ones. Pop stars are melted down often. We have to keep up with the times."

Saying good-bye to the guard, the girls turned towards the House of Horrors.

"It's dark in here," Jo said. "Where are you, Robin?"

"Right here, in back of you. Wait a minute. I've got something in my shoe. I'll have to stop to take it out."

"Eek! No! Agh!"

"What's that noise?" Robin asked. "Jo? Mom?"

No one answered her.

"They must have gone on ahead," Robin said to herself. "I guess they didn't hear me."

Robin walked slowly through the darkness. She could hear footsteps. But she wasn't sure if they were behind her or ahead of her.

"Mom? Jo?" she called again, but there was no answer.

She walked past a recreation of Jack the Ripper's London. The lighting was a little better with tall gas lamps casting a faint glow on the cobblestone street. The sound of horses' hooves on the pavement made her jump. Then she realized it was a recording. Clip, clop, clip, clop. She heard a man jump out of a carriage and start walking on the street.

"Help! Help!" she heard a woman scream. And then the woman stopped screaming, and Robin knew that Jack the Ripper had killed again.

"Wow! That was something," she said. She started walking faster now. There was a long blank stretch before the exit. Most of it was in darkness. Robin stepped into the shadows, and heard the footsteps behind her again.

It seemed like a repeat of the Ceremony of the Keys. When she walked faster, the other person walked faster. She could hear someone breathing close to her.

"Am I going crazy or is this happening again?" she wondered.

Then a boy who seemed to be about ten years old ran past her into the light and looked back at her and grinned.

"Fooled you, fooled you," he yelled. "Bet you thought I was the Ripper coming after you."

Robin leaned against a wall until her knees stopped feeling like jelly. She looked up to see her mother and Jo coming towards her.

"Where were you?" her mother said. "We've been looking all over for you."

"I stopped to fix my shoe. I thought you heard me, but I guess you didn't," Robin said.

"What's the matter? You're pale and you look shaky," her mother said.

"See that little kid over there? He really scared me. He stalked me in the darkness."

"Someone ought to talk to his mother about scaring people," Mrs. Bridge said.

"Never mind, Mom. I'm all right now." Robin started walking towards the door.

"I think you need some air," their mother said. "And I've got just the place."

She motioned them towards a red double-decker bus and the three of them climbed to the top. There the girls were delighted to be sitting in the open air looking at the sights all around them, as the bus carried them to the London Zoo.

"Everything's so green," Jo said.

"And it's green even in winter," their mother said.

"How could that be? Isn't it cold here in the winter?" Robin asked.

"Yes, but very often it rains, and it's the moisture that keeps things green."

By the time they finished looking at the elephants, zebras, and tigers, not to mention two rhinos called Rosie and Jos, the Bridges were drooping.

"How about some tea?" their mother asked.

"You know we don't drink it," said Jo.

"No, I mean British tea, that is, a four o'clock snack."

"Now you're talking," Robin said.

They sat down at an outdoor table near a fountain.

"I'll get us something to eat," their mother said.

"What happened at Madame Tussaud's?" Jo asked.

"I thought I was going crazy. I started hearing footsteps again like at the Ceremony of the Keys."

"But it was only a little kid, right?"

"Right. But I was thinking. Maybe we need some help with this."

"Like who. Mom?"

"No, but maybe Vivian could help. I mean he's English and everything. He'll know what to do."

"I don't think being English makes him any better at catching the Ripper than we'd be," Jo said.

"I didn't mean that. It's a big responsibility. I guess I got carried away, thinking we could do it alone."

"We can do it alone. I don't think we need a boy to help us."

"Vic's not a boy, he's a friend."

Jo looked at Robin and laughed.

"Well, you know what I mean," Robin said.

"Look, we hardly know him. I mean we just met him yesterday.

What makes you think he won't go running to tell Mom? Then we won't be able to do anything on our own."

"Vic's not like that," Robin said.

"How do you know?" Jo asked.

"How do you know what?" Mrs. Bridge asked, carrying a tray of tea, soft drinks, and cakes.

Robin looked around desperately for something to give her an idea of what to say. She saw ducks waddling around picking up pieces of bread from the grass.

"How do I know it's not safe to feed the ducks," she said.

"How do you know?" their mother asked.

"It says so in Jo's guidebook. I guess they snap at you."

"That sounds like good advice. I think after this we'll go back and have a nap at the B&B before we go out to dinner tonight."

"I'm not tired," Jo said. "Robin and I can hang out here and go back later."

"No, you're coming back with me. No hanging out alone in a strange city. This isn't home. Let's go."

Riding back on the Underground, Robin couldn't wait to see whether anyone had disturbed the traps she had set in their room. When they reached the B&B, she raced upstairs ahead of her mother and came to a dead stop when she saw the handle of their door.

"Jo! The hairs are gone!"

Jo examined the door handle.

"You're right. Let's see if the powder's still there."

They walked over to the windowsill and looked down. The powder was completely gone. And there were no footprints.

"Look behind the curtain!"

"I'm almost afraid to," said Robin. She pulled back the curtain. The case was still there.

"This is creepy," Jo said. "The hair and the powder are gone but the Ripper left no traces."

"We're up against somebody really clever," Robin said.

Just then Mrs. Bellaqua stuck her head into the room.

"Oh, girls, just a word. Could you be careful how you use your powder? We vacuum the rooms every day, and it's hard to get it out of the carpet. Ta, luvs."

CHAPTER SIX

The Mystery of Simon

"Whew! That's a relief," said Robin. "No Ripper, just a very clean B&B owner."

"Maybe the Ripper doesn't know we have the knives," Jo said.

"Then who followed me at the Ceremony of the Keys?" asked Robin.

"It could be just a coincidence," Jo said.

"It could be. But I have the feeling someone's watching me all the time," Robin said. "I just can't shake it."

"It must be creepy."

Robin shivered. "It is. I still think we should ask Vic to help us. He knows London. He could help us figure out what to do. Maybe we should turn the knives over to the police."

"And lose all the fun of trying to track down the Ripper ourselves? You can't mean it," Jo said.

"It might be too much for us," Robin said, slowly.

"I don't think so," Jo said. Then she looked at her sister and added, "All right. If you want to tell Vic, it's okay. Maybe he'll have some ideas. But I'm not turning the knives over to the police. Where's your spirit of adventure? You're the mystery fan. I thought this would be right up your alley."

"Okay," Robin said, "I just thought it might be too dangerous for..."

"For who?"

"For you," Robin said.

"You mean you think I'm a baby," Jo said, stamping her foot. "Stop treating me like a two year old. I'm just as good as you are at solving mysteries."

"Of course. I was just worried about you. Mom would kill me if anything happened to you."

"You just take care of yourself," Jo said. "Don't worry about me." She stalked over to the window and pulled down the case. Throwing it open, she gazed at the knives again. She picked one up and examined it closely.

"Look, there are little grooves on the knives," she said. "I wonder what they are?"

"Let's see if the newspaper says anything about it," Robin said. She unfolded the paper they had bought in Leicester Square.

"Six victims...all in the eastern United States...oh, here it is," she said.

"What?" cried Jo. She looked over her sister's shoulder.

"He marks his kills with notches in the knives."

"Ugh!" Jo wrinkled her nose. "That's disgusting."

Robin examined the knives again.

"There are six notches here, but there's something funny about them," she said. "There's a space after the first three."

Jo picked one up. "Yes, I see what you mean. Why would he do that?"

"Maybe it's his own strange system," said Robin. "Let's put the case back up in the window. No one's found it so far."

"Unless Mrs. Bellaqua decides to wash the windows," Jo said.

Robin rubbed her finger over the windowpane.

"It looks pretty clean to me. I'd say we're safe for a while. Meantime, let's be on the lookout for anyone suspicious. I still get the feeling that someone's following me."

"Okay. I'll make sure to look around."

Just then a knock on the door made them both jump.

"Who is it?" called Robin.

"It's your mother. Who else would it be?"

Robin opened the door.

"Did you have a nice nap?" their mother asked.

"Sure," Robin said.

"But you haven't changed. Hurry up, we don't want to be late for Vic's uncle."

After they had changed, the girls ran downstairs to find their mother talking to Mrs. Bellaqua.

"I'll give you that guidebook for the Globe tomorrow. I have to hunt it up. My son took it and I don't know where he put it. You must be happy you have two nice, quiet girls. They're probably no bother at all." Mrs. Bellaqua sighed. "There's always something with boys. My son's grown now, but he gave us quite a bit of trouble when he was younger."

"Does he live here with you?" Mrs. Bridge asked.

"He travels about. He was in the States, but he's come home for a short visit. Ah, here he is now."

A slim, dark man wearing a black leather jacket came through the passage. He scowled when he saw Mrs. Bellaqua.

"Where are you going, Simon?"

"Out. Don't wait up. I'll be back late."

"This is Mrs. Bridge and her two daughters. They're staying with us for a while."

He gave them a mocking smile and a bow, then slipped out the door.

"I'll say good-bye now. We'd better be going, otherwise we'll be late for dinner," Mrs. Bridge said.

"Cheerio," said Mrs. Bellaqua, looking worriedly out of the window after her son.

Robin was quiet while her sister chattered with her mother on the Underground train.

After they left the Underground and walked down the street, Mrs. Bridge turned to Robin. "What's the matter, Robin? Aren't you feeling well?" Before Robin could stop her, her mother felt her forehead.

"No fever. Does your stomach hurt?"

"I'm fine, Mom. I'm just thinking. Do I have to talk all the time for you to think I'm all right?"

"It's not like you to be so quiet. I was worried."

"I'm okay. Look, here's Vic's uncle's restaurant."

As they walked through the sliding door, Jo whispered, "What's up?"

"I just had another thought," Robin whispered back. "Tell you later."

Uncle Peter walked towards them, rubbing his hands. Vic was behind him.

"Ah! Here are the Bridges. Ready for some nice raw fish, Jo?"

"Um, er..." Jo stammered.

Uncle Peter laughed. He and Mrs. Bridge introduced themselves.

"Is your husband here with you?" he asked.

"I'm sorry. He went to Bath for a conference. I hope you'll meet when he comes back."

"I'm sure we will. Now let's sit down. Unfortunately, my sushi chef still hasn't arrived, so we'll have to have cooked food. I'm sure Jo will be disappointed."

Jo's face lit up when she tasted the grilled steak with teriyaki sauce and the white rice.

"This tastes like the food at home."

"I hope you like it," Uncle Peter said. "I just wish my sushi chef would show up. I can't imagine what happened to him."

"Do you think he's lost?" Mrs. Bridge asked.

"I gave him clear directions in Japanese to this place. He knows very little English, so I am a bit worried. If Mr. Ogawa doesn't show up in another day, I'll call the police, although I'd rather not."

"Why? Won't the police help?" Robin asked.

"That's not the problem. Mr. Ogawa is terrified of the police. He had some trouble with immigration the first time he came here, and to him, it's all the same thing. Anyone in a uniform is upsetting to him."

"It must be hard to be in a strange country and not speak the language," Mrs. Bridge said.

"Yes, I felt the same way the first time I went to New York," Uncle Peter said. "You know, in England, a bathroom is a room where you take a bath. Every time I asked for the loo, no one knew what I meant."

"Not to mention football," Vic said.

"What do you mean?" Robin asked.

"Our football is your soccer," he said.

"Never mind that," said Mrs. Bridge. "What about your cockney slang? Nobody could ever figure that out."

"What's that?" Jo asked.

"It's a sort of rhyming code," Uncle Peter explained. "The Cockneys—that is anyone who lives in a certain part of London, within the sound of the Bow Church bells—made up a slang so that outsiders wouldn't know what they were talking about."

"Do you know any?" asked Robin.

"Sure. There are a few words that everybody knows," he said. "Take the word wife, for example. The Cockneys call her 'trouble and strife.'"

"What else?" Robin asked, eagerly.

"Why don't you guess? I'll tell you the Cockney and you see if you can figure it out. Here's one: 'plates of meat.'"

"Plates of meat," Robin said. She wrinkled her brow and thought. Then she noticed Vic smiling and pointing down at his shoes.

"Feet!" she cried.

"Very good," said Uncle Peter. "Here's another one: 'Hampstead Heath.' It's another part of the body."

"Teeth!" yelled Jo.

"Here's a harder one: 'apples and pears.'"

"Ears?"

"No."

Mrs. Bridge smiled. "I know this one."

"Tell, Mom," said Jo. "I can't figure this one out."

"Stairs," she said.

"That's right," Uncle Peter said. "And now here's the sweet."

"What's that?" asked Jo.

"Ice cream," said Uncle Peter, and everyone laughed. He brought the shiny black dishes to the table himself.

"It's green," said Jo. "Is it pistachio?"

"You tell me," he said. "Taste it."

"It doesn't taste like pistachio, but it's good," she said.

"It's made with green tea," said Vic.

"You're kidding," said Jo, as she ate another spoonful.

"No, really. I didn't want to eat it the first time Uncle Peter told me what it was, but then I tried it. Now it's one of my favorite desserts."

"Not something the butler usually serves for pudding, eh, Vic?" Uncle Peter said.

Vic looked embarrassed and mumbled something.

Jo gave him a sharp look. Then she said, "Ice cream made with tea, tandoori chicken. I sure am eating some strange things. But I like them."

"If I have nothing else to thank you for, that would be enough," Mrs. Bridge said to Uncle Peter.

"Ah, but wait until Jo tries raw eel," he said.

"Never!" Jo cried.

After they finished, Robin and her mother walked to the door, but Jo lingered as Vic talked to his uncle for a minute.

"Haven't you told them?" Jo heard Uncle Peter ask. "Why not?"

"Americans don't look at these things the same way," Vic said. "Besides, I'd like to forget all that nonsense."

"Come on, Jo," Robin called. "Let's go."

Vic walked them back to the Underground. He pointed out the small Chinese shops filled with mysterious powders and herbs and the restaurant windows hung with roasted ducks and spareribs.

"Not much like home," Mrs. Bridge said.

"What is Westbrook, New Jersey, like?" Vic asked.

Robin tried to tell him about the streets lined with tall trees, the green lawns, and the big houses. She described her sprawling school with its huge gym and auditorium. Then she told him about the shopping malls and what she and friends liked to do on the weekends.

"It doesn't sound that different from where I live, except everything in England is much smaller," Vic said.

"Maybe we can see your house someday," Jo said.

"Maybe." Vic didn't sound so sure.

"Here comes the train. Will we see you tomorrow?" Robin asked.

"Sure. I'll come to the B&B in the morning."

"I want to go to the Globe Theatre tomorrow," their mother said. "Why don't you come with us, Vic?"

He nodded yes and waved good-bye as the train pulled into the station.

"We never told him," Robin whispered to Jo.

"Maybe we shouldn't. I think there's something strange about him," Jo whispered back.

"You're strange," said Robin, in disgust.

"What are you girls buzzing about?" Mrs. Bridge asked.

"Nothing," Jo said. "Here's our stop."

The girls ran up the stairs to their room, while Mrs. Bridge stopped to get the guidebook Mrs. Bellaqua had promised.

"Wait!" Robin stopped Jo from going inside. The door was open and they could see a man moving inside their room. The man reached up to touch the green curtains hiding the case.

"Who's there?" Robin called.

The man jumped. He turned around and came to the door. It was Mrs. Bellaqua's son, Simon.

"Just changing the towels in your room. My Mum said you needed some fresh ones," he said.

"But we just got some new towels—Ow!" Jo yelled.

"Thank you," said Robin.

"No problem," Simon said. He cast another look at the green curtains and then left the room reluctantly.

"Why did you pinch me?" Jo asked Robin, rubbing her arm.

"Because I wanted him to think we believed him. Obviously, he wasn't in our room because he was bringing us towels."

"Why do you think he was here?"

"I had this idea going to the restaurant. Mrs. Bellaqua told us that her son was in the U.S. for a while, and now he's here. She said they had some trouble with him."

"So?"

"So it occurred to me that the case of knives didn't get here by accident."

"And?"

"And what if Simon Bellaqua is the Ripper?"

CHAPTER SEVEN

The Mystery of the Missing Jewels

 "It makes perfect sense," Robin said to Jo. "I didn't really pick up the wrong case at the airport. Instead, Simon switched cases so he could hide the knives."

"Why would he do that?" Jo asked. "He'd know we'd look inside."

"Maybe he thought he'd be able to get the case before we looked. Anyway, he probably thought that we're only kids, he could fool us."

"Maybe," said Jo.

"It does explain why I feel as if someone's watching me all the time. Simon can follow us wherever we go. And he knows we're always going to come back here at night."

"Now you're giving me the creeps," Jo said. "What if he breaks in here at night?"

"We'll jam the chair under the doorknob again. He won't be able to get in without making a lot of noise."

"How are we going to stop him from coming into the room tomorrow when we're out and taking the knives?" Jo asked.

"We'll hide the case in a different spot," Robin said. She looked around.

"I've got it," she said. She took the case of knives and placed it inside her empty suitcase. Then she pushed the suitcase to the back of the small closet.

"Excellent, Sherlock. Now let's sleep on it," Jo said.

Nothing disturbed the girls that night, but in the morning they woke to a terrible commotion.

"My pearls! They're gone. I know I had them," a woman sobbed.

"And I just bought my watch," growled a man. "It's very expensive."

The girls opened their door a crack and peered into the hall. There they saw an American couple talking to Mrs. Bellaqua.

"I don't know what happened to your jewelry," she said, looking worried. "Perhaps you mislaid it?"

"I've looked all over," the woman said. "I even looked under the bed. I can't find my necklace and my husband's watch anywhere."

"Have some breakfast," Mrs. Bellaqua said. "I'll take a look and see if I can find what's missing."

"Why not call the police?" the man asked.

"Give me a minute first," Mrs. Bellaqua said. "I'm sure I can find them. Sometimes things slip down behind the beds."

"All right," said the woman, "we'll have some coffee, but I don't think I could eat a thing."

"I put my watch on the dresser last night. How could it slip down behind the bed?" the man asked as his wife led him away.

The girls watched as Mrs. Bellaqua stood there with her hands on her hips looking grim. Then they saw her beckon to someone hiding in the shadows.

"Put those things back now," she said, sharply.

Jo and Robin gasped as they saw Simon produce the jewelry and slip into the couple's room. As Mrs. Bellaqua turned their way, Robin silently closed the door.

"What was that all about?" Jo asked Robin.

"I don't know, but I'm awfully glad we hid the case. I don't think Simon would dare to look in our closet after this."

"I hope not." Jo shivered. "This is some place Mom and Dad found. Do you think Mrs. Bellaqua steals too?"

"I don't know. She certainly knew that Simon had the stuff. We'd better keep our eyes open. It's a good thing we don't have anything valuable here."

"We'd better tell Mom."

"Right, but only about this, not about the case," Robin said.

"Of course."

At breakfast, they watched as Mrs. Bellaqua produced the missing necklace and watch.

"Here's your jewelry. Just as I said. I moved the bed and there it was."

"I'm sure I put it on the dresser last night," the man insisted.

"Never mind, Sam, I'm just glad it was found. Thank you, Mrs. Bellaqua," the woman said.

Mrs. Bellaqua gave them a thin smile and moved away to bring more toast.

"Ready for the Globe Theatre?" Mrs. Bridge asked.

"We have to wait for Vic," Robin said.

"Of course," her mother said.

They were glad they had as he guided them through the three station changes they needed to make to get to the theater.

"Is it always so complicated to get places?" Jo asked.

"Not really. This isn't so bad. How do you get around when you're home?"

"Mom or Dad usually drives us," Jo said.

"Sometimes we walk or take a bus, but it's harder in the suburbs," Robin said.

"Here we are," said their mother. Robin looked up to see a round building.

"It doesn't look very old," she said.

"That's because it was rebuilt just a few years ago," Mrs. Bridge said. "Let's hurry. It looks like a tour is starting."

While Mrs. Bridge paid for them, Vic and the girls crowded in with a group that threaded its way through narrow hallways into a large room. Robin looked around. There were wooden seats at three levels around the room. The top seats were up near the ceiling, but she didn't see any way to get up there. A young woman with long blonde hair invited them to sit in the seats nearest the ground. In front of those seats was a wide floor that sloped down to the stage. The stage itself was supported by columns and had a roof over it. As Robin moved over to make room for Mrs. Bridge, the guide began to speak: "Welcome to the Globe. There's been a theater on this site ever since 1598. We've recreated the old theater of oak timbers and white plaster. The original had a thatched roof, but our Globe is open to the sky. That's why when it rains, there's no performance."

Robin dozed off through most of the guide's lecture. She woke up when everyone got up to move towards the stage.

"What did I miss?" she asked Vic.

He grinned as she rubbed her eyes. "Not much," he said. "There was a lot about Shakespeare, but I was wool-gathering myself."

The guide continued, "The members of the audience who stood in front of the stage were called groundlings, naturally, because they stood on the ground throughout the performance. They were also called stinkers. Does anyone know why?"

The crowd looked puzzled. Smiling, the guide said, "First, they were standing on a floor that was made up of crushed hazelnuts and dirt from the Thames River. In those days, everyone threw their garbage into the river so you can imagine what the dirt smelled like. Another reason is that the Elizabethans—people who lived when Elizabeth the First was queen—weren't shy. They used the groundling pit—as it was called—as a loo—or bathroom, as you Americans would say. That's why the floor was built to slope downwards. There were holes there that drained into the river. Now that you can imagine what the Globe smelled like, let me tell you..."

"That was cool!" Jo whispered to Robin. "I can't wait to tell my friends about it. Imagine, the theater was a bathroom."

"Ugh! I can't imagine it. But it's more interesting than what she was talking about before. I couldn't keep my eyes open."

"Speaking of keeping our eyes open, have you told Vic yet?" Jo asked.

"No," said Robin. She looked around. Her mother had gone to the front of the stage and was listening to the guide intently.

She waved to Vic and he came over.

"I've got something to tell you," she whispered. Quickly, before her mother noticed, she led Vic out of the theater door and into the lobby. Two ladies sat talking there under a sign about donations for the theater. Otherwise, no one was around. Speaking fast, Robin filled Vic in on the discovery of the knives, their traps, and Simon and the jewels.

"Wow! Are you sure you haven't been reading too many thrillers?" Vic asked. "Nothing exciting like that ever happens in England."

"If you think I'm making it up, I'll show you the knives," Robin said. She glared at him as if daring him not to believe her.

"Oh, I believe you, all right," Vic said, backing away. "It's just I've never, ever had anything like this happen to me."

"I never had it happen to me either," Robin said. "Now I'm not sure what to do. Should we call in Scotland Yard?" Her eyes sparkled at the idea.

"And say what? You found a case of knives and you think someone's following you."

"It does sound pretty lame," Robin said. "What about Simon and the jewels and Mrs. Bellaqua?"

"That sounds more like it, but I don't know how it ties in with the Ripper. Is he a jewel thief, too?"

"I don't think so. I don't remember reading anything like that."

"I think first on our list should be to find out more about Simon and Mrs. Bellaqua," Vic said. "I'll come back with you, and we'll try to see what's going on. That's the only thing Scotland Yard would be interested in, and if we can find some kind of proof that he's the Ripper, that would be great!"

The crowd started streaming out of the lobby. Mrs. Bridge was in front holding Jo by the arm.

"Robin, where were you? I can't believe you left in the middle of the talk. It was so interesting."

"I'm sorry, Mom, I...I..."

"She had the hiccups, Mrs. Bridge. I helped her find some water." Vic beamed at Robin's mother.

"Oh, well, that's different. But I am sorry you missed the rest of the talk. There were a lot of interesting facts. She said there was a bear-baiting pit right next door to the Globe. Shall we try to find it?"

"Sure, Mom," Robin said.

They walked outside to a terrace that overlooked the Thames.

"Look," Mrs. Bridge said, "that's St. Paul's Cathedral. We should go there."

They all gazed across the river at the skyline of central London, the wide buildings squatting on the opposite bank like large gray frogs. Then they walked through huge, black, wrought-iron gates and onto a narrow path.

"I don't see any bears," Jo said.

"They're not here now," Mrs. Bridge said. "This was hundreds of years ago. I just want to see where they were. Let's turn up this way."

Much to her delight, they came upon a sign that said "Bear Lane."

"Look, girls, can you imagine it? People would be crowding around a bear chained to a pole. The bear would fight a pack of dogs, and people would bet on who would win."

"It sounds awful," Jo said. "Didn't they get hurt?"

Mrs. Bridge seemed to come back to reality.

"Yes, it was terribly cruel. Life was different then. You heard about that in the Globe."

"I'm glad I live today," Jo said.

"Me too," Robin said. "I can't imagine hurting an animal."

"Me three," said Vic.

"You're right," Mrs. Bridge said. "Sometimes the historian in me gets carried away. Let's do something modern."

"How about going to Hamley's?" Vic said.

"What's that?" Robin asked.

"The biggest toy store in the world." Vic grinned. "Really, it's lots of fun."

"Fine," said Mrs. Bridge. She walked down to inspect the end of the lane more closely.

"It sounds babyish," Robin said.

"Oh, come on, Robin, don't be a spoilsport," Jo said.

"It'll give us a chance to talk on our own and plan what to do about Simon," Vic said to the girls. "You'll see, it's the perfect place."

"All right," Robin said. "Let's go."

CHAPTER EIGHT

The Mystery of Agatha Christie

 Robin saw what Vic meant the minute they entered the store on Regent Street. The street was lined with clothing shops for men and women and china and jewelry shops. But there was only one toy store. Hamley's was crammed with children of various ages running from toy to toy. Downstairs, buzzers, bells, and children's shrieks were ringing noisily in the electronics department.

Mrs. Bridge's mouth dropped open. "Even in the States at Christmas I've never seen anything like this," she said.

"It goes on all the time," Vic shouted to her. "Isn't it fun?"

She smiled weakly at Vic.

Jo pulled on her arm. "Come on, Mom, let's go look at some of the handheld games." She dragged her towards the electronic toy area, and they disappeared on a wave of buzzing coming from a pinball machine.

"I promised Jo I'd fill her in later, if she took care of Mom," Robin said.

"Good thinking."

They walked over to a display of Paddington Bear toys. Robin fiddled with the bear's yellow slicker while they talked.

"How can we find out more about Simon and Mrs. Bellaqua?" she asked.

"Maybe you could ask how long he was in the States," Vic said.

"After all, as an American that would be a perfectly natural thing to ask. Then you could try to find out where he was. Then we'll see if the dates and the cities match up to the Ripper's murders."

"Excellent," said Robin. "I'll do it the minute we get back."

"I'll help you," Vic said. "Are you telling your mother about this?"

"I think we have to," Robin said. "Jo and I have each other, but she's alone now that my father's away. I wouldn't want her to catch Simon in her room."

"Let's talk to her after we talk to Mrs. Bellaqua and figure out a few things. Then it'll make more sense," said Vic.

"Gotcha. Oops, here comes Mom. Look busy."

Robin studied Paddington with great interest, while Vic drifted over to the board games.

"I guess you're never too grown up for Paddington Bear," Mrs. Bridge announced as she came towards Robin. She pushed her hair back from her forehead. "I, however, have had it. I've heard more bells, whistles, and beeps than I've ever heard before, or ever wish to again. Get your sister, Robin, if you can drag her away from all the electronic games. I'm ready to go."

Robin ran to get Jo and explained everything she and Vic had talked about.

"We have to go back to the B&B now so let's tell Mom we're tired," Robin said.

"I hope she'll believe us. She knows we never get tired," Jo answered.

"I think Hamley's did her in," said Robin, smiling. "At least, I hope it did."

"Nonsense." Mrs. Bridge looked at her watch when the girls said they were tired. "It's not even three o'clock yet. You girls are probably tired because you're hungry. We forgot to have lunch."

"Who needs lunch after that huge breakfast," Robin said.

"I guess that's why I didn't feel hungry around noon the way I usually do," Mrs. Bridge said. "Where can we go for a snack, Vic?"

"We could go to Uncle Peter's," Vic said.

"I think we've imposed on him enough," said Mrs. Bridge. "How about tea? Let's go to Harrods. I heard they have a delicious tea."

"It's a bit pricey," said Vic, looking embarrassed.

"It's my treat," said Mrs. Bridge. "After all, we're on vacation, or holiday as you British say. It's this way, isn't it?" She started walking up Regent Street.

About forty-five minutes later, they reached Harrods and walked through the famous Food Halls. Robin and Jo groaned as they passed counters filled with hard candies, chocolates, pastries, and jams.

"All of a sudden, I'm starved," said Robin to Vic.

"They do have wonderful food here. My mother took me here for lunch once when she was in town."

"Can we meet your mother?" Jo asked. "Where does she live? What does your father do?"

"Ah, here we are now at the restaurant," Vic said. "Let's see if we can get in. Sometimes they're completely booked for tea."

"Tea for four. Certainly, Madame. This way." A smiling man in a long, dark coat led them to a table covered with a snowy white cloth and a silver vase with pink rosebuds.

"We were lucky," Vic said.

"Tea for four," Mrs. Bridge ordered.

They relaxed and looked around as they waited for their meal.

"I think there must be people here from every country in the world," Robin said.

"Harrods is famous," Vic remarked.

Robin frowned.

"What's the matter?" her mother asked.

"I just saw someone who looks familiar," she said. "That Japanese man who just came in reminds me of someone. I can't think who."

Mrs. Bridge looked at the man as he walked past their table.

"Yes, I think I've seen him some place before, too. Maybe in your uncle's restaurant, Vic?"

Vic examined the man carefully as he was led to a table for one. "I don't think so. I know a lot of Uncle Peter's regulars, and I don't think I've ever met him."

"Your tea, Madame."

"Look, I've never seen three-decker sandwiches like this before," Jo said.

Two silver stands were placed before them. Each stand had three levels, and tiny sandwiches stuffed with cheese, tomatoes, watercress, and salmon rested on them. Next, the waiter placed a platter of doughy buns, jam, and whipped cream on the table along with slices of chocolate and raisin cakes and pastries. Finally, he arranged silver pots of steaming tea and bowls heaped with lumps of brown and white sugar in the middle of the table.

"Wow! I always thought tea was just for when you were sick, but this is amazing," Jo said. She picked up one of the doughy buns.

"What's this?" she asked.

"A scone," said Vic. "They're originally from Scotland, but everybody in England eats them."

Jo bit into it. "They're okay, I guess."

"No, no, here's how you eat them," Vic said. He cut the scone in half with a knife and spread a layer of raspberry jam on one of the halves. Then he topped it with a spoonful of the cream and took a bite.

Jo did the same. When she popped a piece of the scone into her mouth, she rolled her eyes in bliss.

"Mmm! That's the best thing I've eaten here. Mom, can we have scones at home?"

"I'm sure I can find a mix or something and make them," Mrs. Bridge said.

While they ate, musicians played the harp and the piano.

Mrs. Bridge sighed. "This is wonderful. But tomorrow I have to get to work. I've taken too much time off as it is. It's the British Museum for us, girls."

"Oh, no, Mom!" cried Jo. "I don't want to be shut up in that stuffy old museum all day."

"What else would you do? You know we said that this was part of the bargain when we were coming to London. You'd have to spend a few days with me at the museum, and when your father comes back, he'll take you around," Mrs. Bridge said.

"How about if they go someplace with me?" Vic asked. "I can take them to see some sights while you're working. We could go to see the Changing of the Guard at Buckingham Palace."

"Do you really have the time?" Mrs. Bridge asked. "Don't your parents want you home, Vic? It's awfully kind of you, but I'd think they want to see you."

"I arranged to spend the week here," Vic said. "I'm staying with Uncle Peter so it's perfectly all right if I spend my time with Robin and Jo. In fact, otherwise I'd be underfoot at Uncle Peter's and a dreadful nuisance."

Mrs. Bridge smiled at Vic. "It's very nice of you to volunteer to take the girls around."

"Say yes, Mom," Jo said. "Please, please."

Robin held her breath.

"All right. But you must be back at the B&B by five every day."

"That's fine," Robin said. "You can count on us, Mom."

"Let's take a bus back," Jo said. "I'm tired of walking. My feet still hurt."

They left Harrods and climbed to the top of another double-decker bus. Robin and Vic sat in front and Mrs. Bridge and Jo found seats directly behind them. As they passed a small statue surrounded by groups of young people, Vic said, "That's Piccadilly Circus."

"Is it famous?" Robin asked.

"Mostly as a meeting place for people."

Robin looked at the bright neon signs and the thick crowds trying to make their way across the streets.

"It looks like Times Square in New York. We've been there a couple of times."

"I guess I'd better go back to Uncle Peter's," Vic said. "It's getting late."

"Okay," Robin said, then added in an undertone, "I'm sorry you couldn't go back to the B&B with us, but Jo and I'll try to find out as much as we can."

"Don't do too much," Vic said. "Wait for me."

"Of course," Robin said. "We'll just scout the scene a little."

"Here's my stop. I'll see you tomorrow." Vic swung off the bus and waved to the Bridges as the bus rumbled and lurched on its way again.

"What shall we do now?" Mrs. Bridge asked.

"I'm not hungry," Jo said. "Not after that enormous tea."

"Neither am I," said Robin. "Do you want to go to a movie?"

"I have a better idea," said their mother. "Get ready to get off the bus." They jumped off at the next stop, and their mother led them through a maze of narrow, twisted streets.

"Where are we going?" Jo asked her mother.

"It's a surprise," she said.

Robin looked around as they walked. The streets were lined with stores and restaurants. Now and then they crossed a cobblestone street, their shoes gripping the curves of the worn, gray stones. She couldn't imagine where they were going.

Suddenly, Mrs. Bridge stopped in front of a small theater. On the marquee was the title *The Mousetrap*.

"Do you have three tickets for tonight?" she asked the man in the booth.

"You're in luck, Madame. I do have three seats for tonight in the balcony, only they're not together. Is that suitable?"

"What do you think, girls?"

"About what?" Jo and Robin asked together.

"This is a famous play. It's a mystery by Agatha Christie, and it's been running at this theater for years and years. Would you like to see it?"

"Oh, yes," said Robin. Jo nodded her head.

"We have about a half an hour before the play starts," Mrs. Bridge said. "Let's get a soda someplace."

After having their soft drinks, the Bridges went back to the theater and walked in.

"Look, we can leave our sweaters there," Jo said, as she pointed to an arrow and a sign that said "Ladies' Cloakroom." But when she followed the arrow she was disappointed to find it was the bathroom.

"Programs!" A woman dressed in black with a white apron held programs in her hand.

"I'll take one," Robin said.

"That'll be sixpence," the woman said.

"Oh, I didn't know you had to pay for it," said Robin. Her mother handed her a coin and she bought one.

They climbed the narrow stairs to their red plush seats in the balcony.

"You and Robin can sit together," their mother said. "I'll be over here in the next row."

Robin and Jo spent the time before the curtain went up looking at the playbill and the other people in the theater. They were interested to see that there were women selling candy and ice cream to the audience. After the curtain rose, both girls became so engrossed in the play that they were surprised when it was intermission.

"What a great mystery," said Jo. "I can't believe all these people are trapped together in one room, and one of them's a murderer."

"How do you like it so far, Robin?" their mother said.

"I love it," she said. "I can't guess the ending. Can you?"

"No. In the ads for the play, they ask you not to tell anybody what the ending is. It must be a real surprise."

The Bridges walked downstairs to stretch their legs. All around them, men and women were drinking and smoking, gathering their drinks from little ledges around the bar.

At the end of the play, Robin and Jo applauded wildly.

"I was really surprised," said Jo.

"Me, too," said Robin, "and I read a lot of mysteries. I should have guessed the ending. I'm going to buy some Agatha Christie mysteries while I'm here. She's really good."

"Let's leave that for another time," their mother said. "I'm dying to get back to the B&B and go to sleep. It's been a long day."

All of a sudden, Robin remembered they hadn't told their mother anything about Simon and the jewels. Was now a good time? She thought about it rapidly. If they told their mother now, would she let them go out with Vic alone the next day?

She made a quick decision, pulling Jo behind her mother as they crossed the street.

"Let's not tell Mom now about Simon," she whispered. "Otherwise, she might not let us go out tomorrow."

"But what if Simon comes into her room in the middle of the night?"

"Do you think it's likely?" Robin asked. "She really has nothing he would want to steal, if he's just a thief. I mean she doesn't have any jewels or anything like that."

"Do you think he knows that?"

"He must have cased the place," Robin said.

"But we found him in our room," Jo said. "He knows we don't have anything valuable."

"I guess we'd better tell her," Robin said. "Maybe she won't go berserk if we tell her in the right way."

"What way is that?" asked Jo.

"I don't know," admitted Robin. "I've never been able to figure it out."

Jo didn't answer. She just held up her fingers and crossed them for luck.

CHAPTER NINE

The Mystery of the Tea Party

 Robin planned what she would say to her mother. First, she would tell her what she and Jo had seen. Then she would emphasize that they were in no danger. After that, she would assure her mother that they would be all right going to Buckingham Palace with Vic the next day.

They reached the quiet, tree-lined square where their B&B was before Robin felt ready to say something. Jo kept poking her to speak and she finally got up her nerve.

"Mom, there's something I have to tell you."

Her mother stopped dead in her tracks.

"What's wrong?"

"Nothing's really wrong, but Jo and I, well, we—"

Before Robin could say anything more, the door of the B&B opened and Mrs. Bellaqua stood there looking at them.

"Oh, Mrs. Bridge. Did you enjoy your day out?"

"It was lovely, thank you, Mrs. Bellaqua."

"I'm just waiting up for my son, Simon, and I thought I heard someone outside. I didn't realize it was you."

"I'm sorry we disturbed you," Mrs. Bridge said.

"No bother at all. In fact, I was about to put on the kettle. Would you care for a cup of tea?"

"You know, I really would appreciate that. There's something about walking around all day that makes you thirsty."

"Would you girls like some?"

"No thanks," said Robin. She couldn't wait to get away from Mrs. Bellaqua.

"Mom, are you sure you want some tea?" she asked. "Won't it keep you up?"

"Robin, I don't think anything will keep me up. I could use something to drink, though. But didn't you want to tell me something?"

Robin felt Mrs. Bellaqua staring at her.

"It was nothing. Just be careful."

"What do you mean?" Mrs. Bridge asked.

"It's always good to be careful," she said.

"I guess my ideas are finally getting across to you," Mrs. Bridge said. She turned to Mrs. Bellaqua. "Sometimes I think they don't listen to me, but I guess it is sinking in."

"Don't I know it," said Mrs. Bellaqua. "I've been through that myself. Now come along, and we'll have that cup of tea. You'll feel better after that."

"Goodnight, girls. Sleep tight." Mrs. Bridge kissed her daughters and went down to the breakfast room with Mrs. Bellaqua.

"Why didn't you say something?" hissed Jo.

"What could I say? She was standing right there," Robin answered.

"What do we do now?" Jo asked.

"We'll have to keep watch on Mom to make sure she's all right. We don't want Mrs. Bellaqua poisoning her."

"Do you think she would?" Jo asked.

"Who knows?"

"Now you're scaring me," said Jo. "She wouldn't hurt Mom, would she?"

"Let's make sure she doesn't," Robin said. She motioned to Jo to take off her shoes, and they tiptoed down the stairs to the breakfast room.

"Stop," Robin whispered. She held out her hand to make sure Jo stayed on the stair step above her. Then she crouched down, hidden by the staircase, and watched Mrs. Bellaqua and her mother.

"What are they doing?" whispered Jo.

"Drinking tea."

"Does Mom look okay?"

"Yes," said Robin. "She looks fine."

"So the tea isn't poisoned."

"I guess not. Shush now, I want to try and hear what they're saying."

Robin listened intently. It seemed as if all Mrs. Bellaqua was doing was talking about her son. Mom nodded now and then as she sipped her tea.

"...always been a problem. If his father had lived, things would have been different...."

A creak on the stairs made Robin stop listening and sit up. Then she heard footsteps.

"Someone's coming," whispered Jo.

"I know," Robin whispered back. "But there's no place to go."

Both girls tried to shrink back into the shadows. Maybe the person coming down the stairs might not see them in the darkness.

Soft footsteps sounded behind them. Jo clutched Robin's sweater. The footsteps stopped behind them.

"What have we here?" drawled a British voice. It was a man. He bent down towards them. Robin gasped. In the dim light, she could see it was Simon.

"Two little mice," he said, laughing. "What are you doing here, little mice?"

The girls were too scared to speak.

"Can't even let out a squeak," he said. "Now what shall we do with mice? What's that rhyme? 'Cut off their tails with a carving knife. Three blind mice.'"

He lurched towards her. Robin froze.

"Simon, is that you?" Mrs. Bellaqua called.

Simon put his finger to his mouth and said, "Shh" to the girls. Then he ran up the stairs away from the breakfast room.

"Simon?"

Robin looked down at the breakfast room again. Mrs. Bellaqua put her head down and started to cry. Mrs. Bridge put her arm around her.

"Let's go," whispered Jo to Robin.

They skittered up the steps, not caring how much noise they made, looking around for Simon. But he had disappeared.

"Thank heavens," Robin said, and they ran up to their room, locked the door and pushed the chair under the knob.

"Wasn't that creepy!" Jo exclaimed.

"I thought I would die when he came down the stairs and said that thing about the mice," Robin said.

"We could have screamed for Mom," Jo said. "She was right there."

"I couldn't have screamed if my life depended on it," Robin

said. "I never knew what it meant to be scared to death before, but I know now."

"What are we going to do?"

"I'm going to wait up for Mom and tell her everything."

"Everything?" Jo asked.

"Well, about Simon anyway," she said.

"I'll wait up with you," Jo said.

But the longer they talked, the more their eyes drooped.

"I'm getting really tired," Jo said.

"We can't go to sleep. We have to tell Mom tonight," Robin said. "Let's go try her room now."

"What if we see Simon again?"

"This time I'll scream," Robin said. "He's not going to scare me again."

They walked over to the staircase and went up to their mother's room.

"Mom!" Robin called softly. No answer.

She knocked on the door. "Mom!" she called more loudly.

A woman's head poked out of the room next door.

"Excuse me! People are trying to sleep here."

"I'm sorry. I was just trying to see if my mother was in her room."

"Are you sick?" the woman asked.

"No," Robin said, "I just want to talk to her."

"Well, talk to her in the morning." The woman slammed her door.

"I don't think she's there," Jo said. "What are we going to do now?"

"We could wait outside her door until she comes up," Robin suggested.

"What if Simon comes along? Do you think he's around here somewhere?" Jo asked.

"I think he went out. We haven't heard him, have we?"

"That's enough." A man in a bathrobe came out into the hall. "How is anyone supposed to get any sleep with you girls chattering in the hall? Aren't you supposed to be in bed?"

"Please, we didn't mean to bother anyone," Robin said. "We'll be quiet. We're just waiting for our mother."

"Your mother went into her room a long time ago," he said. "I heard her door close. With all the whisperings and closings of doors and running of water and chattering in the hallways, I haven't had a wink of sleep since I got into bed at ten o'clock."

"Are you sure our mother's in her room?" asked Jo.

"Do you want me to wake her up?" the man asked.

"No," said Robin. "We'll talk to her in the morning."

"Now shoo! Get back to bed. I don't know what your mother's thinking letting you run around this hotel all night." The man waved his hands angrily at them and watched them as they walked down the hallway.

"She must be asleep," Robin said. "You know how soundly she sleeps when she's tired."

"Yes, a fire engine in the bedroom wouldn't wake her up," Jo said.

"We'll just have to wait till morning to talk to her," Robin said. They reached their room and climbed into their beds.

"Goodnight, Robin."

"Goodnight, Jo. See you in the morning."

Robin dreamed of meeting Simon in the hallway. This time, she looked him in the eye.

"Who's a mouse?" she said.

All of a sudden, Robin had turned into a big, black cat and Simon was a little, gray mouse running from her.

"Don't eat me!" he shrieked.

"It would serve you right," she purred. "You tried to scare me."

"Help! Help!" Simon cried. But it wasn't Simon. It was someone else's voice…It was Jo.

Robin sat up in bed.

"Jo, what's the matter?"

"I was lying here trying to go to sleep when I saw the door-knob turn."

"What!"

"Yes. Luckily, it couldn't turn because the chair was in the way. But I definitely heard someone trying to get in."

"This is just too much. Let's wait until morning and tell Mom. We have to get out of here."

"Can I get into bed with you?" Jo asked.

"Sure."

"What time is it?"

Robin looked at the old watch she kept by her bedside. The brown band was fraying, but the watch still kept good time.

"It's four a.m."

"Only three hours to go. We can wake Mom up at seven."

The two girls huddled in the bed until they saw the gray light of dawn coming through the window.

"I never thought I would be glad to get up so early," Jo said.

Robin rubbed her eyes. "I'm really tired, but we can catch up on our sleep later."

"Yeah, after we get out of here and into someplace safe."

They washed themselves with cold water from the basin to wake themselves up. Neither dared to take a shower alone.

"Aren't you dressed yet?" Robin asked.

"It takes longer when you're tired. I'm almost ready."

Finally, they left their room and ran up the stairs to their mother.

"Mom! Mom!" This time Robin pounded on the door.

The man who had yelled at them last night stuck his head out of the door again.

"Oh, I give up," he said, when he saw who was making the noise.

"She's not answering," Jo said. "Maybe Mrs. Bellaqua did poison her."

Robin pounded harder on the door.

"Mom! Mom, answer us!"

At last, Mrs. Bridge opened the door a crack. She rubbed her eyes hard and groaned.

"Girls, what are you doing up so early?"

"Mom, are you all right?" Jo asked.

"Of course I am. What's gotten into you?"

"I think you'd better let us come in, Mom," Robin said. "We have a lot to tell you."

Mrs. Bridge opened the door wider and Jo practically fell into the room.

"Oh, Mom, I had a terrible night," she cried.

"So did I," said Mrs. Bridge, shaking her head. "So did I."

CHAPTER TEN

The Mystery of the Ripper

 The girls stared at their mother. She had dark circles under her eyes. She ran her hand through her hair.

"Mom, your hair is practically standing straight up from your head," Jo said.

"It's a wonder it's still there," Mrs. Bridge said. "Simon was arrested last night."

"What?"

"Yes, the police came around two a.m. They picked him up for stealing a car."

"A car? Was he trying to make a getaway?" Robin asked.

"I don't know. All Mrs. Bellaqua told me was that he has a history of stealing. Ever since he came back, she's been worried sick about him."

"Stealing?" Robin sat down on Mrs. Bridge's bed with a thump.

"Yes. Why do you look so surprised?"

"We thought he was the Ripper," Jo said, before Robin could warn her not to say anything.

"The Ripper? Why would you think that?"

"No reason," said Robin.

"He just looked like what I imagined the Ripper would look like," Jo said.

Mrs. Bridge shook her head. "The poor woman was hysterical last night. She's been so afraid. She told me she caught him stealing jewelry from the rooms. Of course, she made him put it back."

"We know. We saw him," Jo said.

"What do you mean?"

The girls explained that they had seen Mrs. Bellaqua ordering Simon to put the jewelry back.

"We didn't know what was happening," Robin said. "We thought Mrs. Bellaqua might be a thief, too."

"No, she's as honest as they come. I don't know why her son turned out so bad."

"He was creepy. He caught us on the stairs," Jo said. "We were watching you and Mrs. Bellaqua, Mom. We were afraid she might poison you."

Mrs. Bridge laughed. "No, you can trust her not to poison me. But I'm sorry you were so scared. You see, that's why I don't want you wandering around on your own. Anything could happen."

"The police must have been very quiet," said Robin.

"We didn't see or hear anything. We missed the most exciting part," Jo said.

"I'm glad you did. It was awful. Mrs. Bellaqua was sobbing, and Simon just looked at her with such contempt." Mrs. Bridge shuddered.

"But you're okay, Mom, aren't you?" Jo asked.

"Of course. Just a little tired."

"Do you want to go back to sleep now?" Robin asked.

"No. Maybe we should stay together today. You could come to the British Museum with me."

"Oh, Mom, Vic would be so disappointed. He's counting on showing us the Changing of the Guard at Buckingham Palace."

"Maybe I should go with you."

"Mom, really, we'll be all right," Robin said, in her most grown-up manner. "You can count on me. I'll take care of Jo."

"And I'll take care of Robin," Jo snapped back.

"Okay," Mrs. Bridge sighed. "Let's get dressed and have some breakfast."

A pale Mrs. Bellaqua brought them their hot chocolate and toast.

"How are you this morning?" Mrs. Bridge asked. "Is there anything I can do?"

"Thanks, luv, but it's all well in hand," she said. "It's good to keep busy at a time like this."

She bustled into the kitchen and brought out the plates of eggs and sausage.

Jo smiled up at her. "I hope everything turns out all right," she said.

"You have such sweet girls," Mrs. Bellaqua said. "Take good care of them."

"I try to," Mrs. Bridge said, sighing.

"Hallo." Vic slid into a chair at their table. "Almost ready to go?" As usual, he was wearing his torn green sweater.

Jo poked a finger through one of the holes. "Time to give this to the moths, and get a new one."

"Jo!" Mrs. Bridge glared at her. "That's rude."

"Oh, it's all right," Vic said, smiling. "My mother says the same thing. I just don't care about clothes. I'm like my father that way."

"What does your father do?" Jo asked.

"Nothing special," Vic said. "Come on, we're going to be late if you don't get a push on."

"Take your sweaters, girls," their mother said. "It looks like it's cool out."

"Oh, Mom, do we have to?" Jo whined.

"Yes. Now I'll meet you all back here at five," she said. "Vic, why don't you have dinner with us? We'll pick someplace special."

"Thank you, Mrs. Bridge," he said. "Delighted to."

"I'll get your sweater, Jo," Robin said. "It'll only take me a minute, Vic."

She ran upstairs and raced to their room. Flying down the hall with her head down, she cannoned into a Japanese man who had paused before their room.

"Oof!" Robin ran right into him.

The man backed away, looking fearful.

"Sorry," he said. "So sorry." His thick black hair flopped over his forehead as he bowed to her.

"I'm sorry," Robin said. "It was my fault."

The man sidled off, looking over his shoulder at Robin from time to time.

"He looked scared. I wonder why?" Robin thought.

She would have run after him, but she heard Vic and Jo calling her from downstairs. After grabbing two sweaters and locking the door, she clattered back down the stairs.

"Let's go," said Jo, dancing from foot to foot.

"You're a bouncy bean this morning," Vic said.

"A bouncy bean—what's that?" Jo asked.

"Eager," said Vic.

"Huh?"

"Enthusiastic," said Robin.

"Bouncy bean," Jo said, "I like that." She started to bounce on her toes down the street.

"You'll be sorry you said that," Robin said, as they watched her bounce to the tube station.

"I like Jo. She *is* a bouncy bean," Vic said. "I wish I had a sister like her."

"Do you have any brothers?" Robin asked.

"No, I'm an only child, which is a bit of a problem," Vic said. "My parents are always worrying about my safety."

"But they let you come to London alone," Robin said. "They don't insist they have to be with you all the time, or make you sit in boring museums while they work."

"Gosh, no," said Vic. "But they do—" He broke off as their train slid into the station.

"All aboard for Buckingham Palace!" yelled Jo. People standing on the platform smiled and laughed.

"Sometimes she is just the most embarrassing girl," Robin said, her face turning red.

"Never mind," said Vic, as they pushed onto the crowded train. Separated from Vic and Jo by a sturdy woman holding two shopping bags and a man in a dark suit with an umbrella and a newspaper under his arm, Robin took the time to think about the events of the night before. Something her mother had said was important. What was it? In her mind, she went over what she

remembered. Something about the time. Suddenly, she gasped.
Of course, that was it. She had to tell Jo and Vic.

"Our stop," Vic mouthed to Robin. They made their way through
the wedge of people towards the escalator.

By the moving stairs, a busker was singing.

"Oh, mother make my bed, make it both soft and narrow, for I
have died for love today…"

He strummed his guitar and looked pointedly at his open guitar
case strewn with coins.

Vic threw him a coin.

"Thank you, brother." The busker bowed and finished his song.

As they rode to the top of the stairs, Robin could hardly wait to
tell them what she had realized.

"You'll never believe what—"

"Oh, bother." Vic looked at his watch. "We've only got fifteen
minutes before the Horse Guards. Follow me." Vic was off, moving
swiftly through the crowd, looking for the best place to stand.
Finally, he squirmed into a spot where Robin and Jo could look out
without being blocked by anyone taller standing in front of them.

"Jo," said Robin, "guess what I figured—"

"Shh!" people next to her said.

Horse hooves clattered on the cobblestone street and Robin
looked up to see men dressed in red and black uniforms riding
magnificent horses with shining coats. The crowd pressed closer,
and Robin could see the black and gold gates of the palace and the
stern sentries on guard.

"The Queen's not there today," Vic murmured to the girls.

"How can you tell?" Robin asked.

"Her flag's not flying. When she's in residence, you'll see her flag on the pole."

They watched as the band and the new foot guard marched up, and waited patiently while they exchanged salutes and keys. Finally, the old guard marched away and the band started to play.

The tune seemed familiar to Jo and Robin, and they hummed along. Tum-tum-tum-ti-tum-tum-tum-ti-ti-tum-tum... Then Robin burst out laughing.

"It's from *Mary Poppins*. They're playing 'A Spoonful of Sugar Makes the Medicine Go Down.'"

Vic smiled as the girls sang along quietly.

"They often do that, you know," he said. "My cousin told me that once he went to one of the Queen's tea parties, and the band was there playing Beatles' songs."

"Your cousin went to a party with the Queen!" Jo exclaimed. "What was it like? What was she like?"

"Oh, it was boring and stuffy," Vic said. "Nothing special. The Queen is very nice, of course. But her tea parties aren't much fun."

"You sound as if you've been there yourself," Robin said.

"Well, I did go to one or two when I was much younger," Vic said. "They do that for some of the children, and for charities, of course."

"What children?" Jo demanded.

But the guard was now in place and the crowd was drifting off.

"Time to go," said Vic. "What would you like to do next?"

"I don't know," said Robin. "What do you think we should see?"

"How about the Guards' Museum?"

"What's that?" Jo asked.

"You'll see. It'll be a surprise."

Vic led them to a building filled with some of the same uniforms they had seen the guards wearing.

"If it's just clothes, I don't want to see it," Jo said.

"Wait and see." Vic led them back to another building in front of the museum and watched Jo's face.

"Toy soldiers!" she cried. "Millions of them!"

She and Robin were entranced by the miniature toy soldiers dressed in red coats and black pants and the circus and farm animal sets.

"They have miniatures here from every war the British ever fought," Vic said.

"How did you know about this place?" Robin asked.

"I used to come here when I was a little boy just like them." Vic pointed to two boys, one about six or seven, the other a few years older, who were examining the toys and lining them up.

"Boys! Boys!" A man and a woman who were obviously the boys' parents came over to them.

"May I have one, Mummy, Daddy?" the little boy asked. Then, remembering his manners, he said, "Please."

"Nicely said, Albert," his father remarked. "Here—which one do you want?" He put down the newspaper he was carrying on the counter while he helped his son choose a soldier.

"Look!" Jo came up to them. "I'm going to buy this little soldier to take home. It'll remind me of the Changing of the Guard. But which coins do I need to pay with, Vic?"

While Vic went up to the cashier with Jo, Robin glanced casually at the newspaper headlines.

"RIPPER CAU"

That was all she could see because the paper was folded.

"Excuse me, may I look at your newspaper?" she asked the man.

"Bless me, luv, you can take it," he said, getting into line with his son.

Robin opened the newspaper: "RIPPER CAUGHT IN SCOTLAND."

She turned to the article.

> From our correspondent in Edinburgh.
>
> The man known to millions as the Ripper was captured today in the hills of Scotland. Brandishing a wickedly sharp carving knife from his case, the Ripper tried to stab the officer who approached him, but he was overpowered and brought to the ground after a chase that had lasted six months and had led from large cities in the United States to the Scottish hinterlands.
>
> "At one time, we were sure he was in London," said the head of the metropolitan police, Chief Inspector Mark Thomas. "We were wrong. He completely bypassed us and flew straight to Edinburgh."

Robin put down the newspaper. Jo came prancing up to her.

"I love that soldier. I'm going to put him on the dresser tonight."

Vic took one look at Robin's face.

"What's the matter?"

"I think we've been completely wrong about everything," she said, as she showed them the newspaper.

CHAPTER ELEVEN

The Mystery of the Intruder

 "What does this mean?" Jo asked.

"Those weren't the Ripper's knives," Robin said. "The Ripper hasn't been following us. He's been in Scotland the whole time."

"But then whose knives do we have?" Jo asked.

"I don't know," Robin said.

"Maybe the Ripper had a second set of knives. Maybe we took the first set by mistake."

"I don't think so," Robin said. "Let's look in the newspaper story."

They read the whole story. There was no mention of another set of knives.

"Just because they didn't say it doesn't mean it's not true," Jo said. "Otherwise..."

"Otherwise, what?" Robin asked.

"Otherwise, those knives belong to another killer."

"That seems a bit far-fetched to me," Vic said.

"You haven't been through everything we've been through," Jo said. "It's easy for you to blow this off. But I'm scared." She moved closer to Robin.

"Look, it's way past lunchtime. Let's get something to eat and talk this over," Vic said.

"That's a good idea," Robin said.

"All right," said Jo, "but nothing weird. I'm too upset to eat anything strange."

"We'll have pizza," Vic said. "I know just the place."

They walked through the park, then past Lord Nelson's statue at Trafalgar Square. At the square, Robin thought Jo would chase the pigeons with the other tourists, but she walked quietly by Robin's side, looking down at her feet. In a moment of sympathy, Robin squeezed Jo's hand, and her sister looked up at her gratefully. She realized that this was no longer a game for Jo; the younger girl was frightened.

At last they came to a little pizza place near Leicester Square.

"I'll order for us," Vic said. "What would you like on your pizza—corn, ham?"

Jo shuddered. "How about pepperoni?"

"I don't know what that is, but I'll see if they have it."

He came back with three small pies. One had corn nibblets on top of it. The other two were plain.

"They didn't have pepperoni, so I thought it was best to get them plain."

Robin bit into the pizza. It didn't really taste like the pizzas back home, but she was hungry. In a few minutes, she had finished the whole thing. She saw Jo was still nibbling at hers and hoped she wouldn't say anything about how the pizza was better at home.

"This pizza is—" Jo started to say.

"Delicious. Thank you, Vic." Robin kicked Jo before she could finish what she was going to say.

"So what do you think is happening?" Vic asked.

The girls told him about the previous night and the arrest of Simon.

"And he even tried to get in our room," Jo said. "But we jammed the door with a chair."

Robin shook her head slowly. She hated to upset her sister even more.

"That wasn't Simon."

"What do you mean? Who was it?" Jo asked.

"Simon was arrested about two o'clock in the morning. Remember, Mom told us. Someone tried to get into our room at four a.m. I know because I looked at my watch."

"Maybe your watch was wrong. You could have made a mistake. We were really tired."

"I don't think so," Robin said.

"So you have a case of knives you thought belonged to the Ripper. Now you find out it doesn't. Someone tried to get into your room last night, and now you know it wasn't Simon." Vic looked serious. "I think we'd better try and straighten this out."

"I agree," Robin said. "Let's go back to the B&B and call the police. You'll come with us, won't you, Vic?"

"Rather," Vic said. "Wild horses couldn't drag me away. This is getting exciting. Besides, you might need my help."

"Do you think we should call Mom?" Jo asked. "I'd like to have Mom around."

"We can stop into the British Museum and see if she's there," Robin said. She sighed as she thought of explaining everything to her mother and of how she might never be free to roam around London again.

"Are you really sure you want to bother Mom with this?" she asked, hoping Jo would change her mind.

"Yes," said Jo, "and I think we should have told her in the beginning. Then we wouldn't be wandering around, afraid like this."

"I'm not afraid," Robin said.

"Well, I am," Jo said. "I'm afraid of going back to that horrible B&B and that Mrs. Bellaqua. For all we know, they're her knives, and she's going to come in at night and cut us up."

"Oh, please. Now you're being silly," Robin said.

"Nothing like that ever happens in London," Vic said. "You know, the police aren't even allowed to carry guns here. It's quite peaceful."

Jo started coughing. She couldn't seem to stop.

"I…cough, cough…got something…cough…stuck…"

"I'll get you something to drink," Vic said. He hurried up to the counter.

"Robin," Jo whispered in her ear.

"What happened to your cough?"

"Never mind. Did it ever occur to you that we don't know much about Vic? He never talks about his family. Maybe those knives are his."

"Don't be ridiculous! Vic is a kind, nice person. He's taken all this time to show us around," Robin said indignantly.

"Maybe that was his way of keeping track of us," Jo said. "I think there's something fishy about him."

"Fishy yourself," Robin said. "The idea. He was as surprised about the knives as we were. I can't believe you think he's dangerous."

"I didn't say dangerous. Just keep your eye on him," Jo said.

"I will not."

Vic came back with a cola drink.

"Thank you," Jo said and took a sip.

"Thank you, Vic. That was very kind and thoughtful of you," Robin said. "Now let's go, that is, if you're over your coughing fit, Jo."

"I feel much better now," Jo said, smiling sweetly.

They walked to Leicester Square and took the Underground to High Holborn. All the way there, Robin was busy turning over possible solutions in her mind. Vic couldn't be involved in this. She just knew he couldn't. Robin looked over at him and he smiled back at her. She liked him so much. She couldn't be that wrong about somebody.

When they got out of the station Jo pulled on Vic's sleeve.

"Which way is it to the British Museum?" she asked.

"This way. It's on Great Russell Street."

They climbed the stone steps and Jo burst into the museum, looking in all directions.

"Do you know where she was likely to be?" he asked Robin.

"No, we never asked because we thought we'd meet her back at the B&B."

"I'll ask the guard where the scholars go," he said.

He walked over to an elderly man in a gray uniform and began talking with him in a low voice.

"He usually doesn't remember the people who come in here, but he did remember your mother because of her red hair, and because she stopped to chat with him. She went out a while ago. He doesn't know where, but he's pretty sure she hasn't come back."

"Let's take a look anyway," Robin said.

They roamed through the halls, taking in the wild horse hunts carved into stone and the tombs of the mummies.

"Look, there are even animal mummies," Jo said. "There's a duck, and a crocodile!"

"I hate to say it," said Robin, slowly, "but this place is—

"Cool!" finished Jo.

Vic smiled. "And you haven't even seen the Rosetta Stone yet."

"What's that?" asked Jo.

"Never mind," said Robin, "we have to find Mom. She definitely isn't here. Maybe she went back to the B&B."

"Probably, she was so tired," Jo said. "I bet we'll find her there."

When they got to the B&B everything was quiet. For once, Mrs. Bellaqua wasn't vacuuming.

"Maybe she went to visit Simon in jail," Robin said.

Jo shuddered.

"Let's get the case first and take it to your mother's room," Vic said. "Then you can show her what you're talking about."

Robin ran up the stairs first and took out her key.

"Aaah!"

Jo and Vic heard her yell.

"What's the matter? What's happened?" They nearly tripped

over each other trying to get up the stairs.

Robin stood in the doorway pointing to a Japanese man dressed in a black suit. He was holding the gray case in his hands.

"The door was open. I found him in here," Robin said, pointing to the man.

Instead of looking frightened or embarrassed, the man seemed angry.

"You bad girl," he said to Robin. "You very bad girl."

"I'm calling the police," Robin said. "I'm not hanging around here."

"No," said the man, opening the case. He took out a knife and waved it. "No police."

Robin backed away. Vic tried to shield her.

"You'd better not hurt her. Put those knives away."

"No police," the man cried. He seemed to be getting more and more upset.

"Get Mom, get somebody," Robin said to Jo.

Jo managed to slip away without the man seeing her, and ran down the stairs. As she ran, she bumped smack into Mrs. Bellaqua.

"Here, be careful, luv."

"Oh, Mrs. Bellaqua, please come, there's a man with a knife in our room, and he's trying to kill Robin and Vic," Jo gasped. She clung to Mrs. Bellaqua desperately.

"What?" Mrs. Bellaqua made her go through it all again.

"Please, hurry."

They scurried upstairs. Robin and Vic were still trying to reason with the man holding the knife.

"Hear now, what's all this?" Mrs. Bellaqua surveyed the scene.

"Why it's Mr. What's His Name. You have Room Fourteen. What are you doing here? Put that knife down."

"He doesn't speak much English," Robin said.

The man continued to hold the knife, staring at all of them defiantly.

"What's got into you? I think he's gone barmy," said Mrs. Bellaqua.

The man started to speak in rapid Japanese. Every now and then he said a few words in English. All they understood was "bad girl, very bad girl."

"Oh, dear, I can speak a bit of Italian and French, but no Japanese," said Mrs. Bellaqua. "Do you know what set him off?"

"No," said Robin, watching him cautiously out of the corner of her eye, "we came upstairs and there he was in the room."

"I wanted to call the police, but every time we say it he gets more and more excited," Vic said.

The man waved the knife around. "No police, police no good."

"You see, he goes bonkers every time we suggest it."

"I wish I could speak Japanese," Mrs. Bellaqua said. "I'm sure there's an explanation. He's been a very nice gentleman up to now. He came the day you did. No trouble at all. And very clean and neat."

"Japanese, Japanese," said Vic. "I know. I'll call my uncle. Cross your fingers that he's in."

"Does he speak Japanese?"

"Fluently," Vic said.

"Then do it, luv. I'd rather not have the police either. Maybe we can do something if we know what he's saying."

Vic tried to leave the room.

The man gestured. "No police. Stay here."

"No police," Vic said. "Calling my uncle. Peter Mountjoy."

"Ah," said the man, his eyes lighting up. "Call. You call."

"He seems to know him," Vic said. "I'll be right back."

The man sank down on the bed. He cradled the knives. Now and then he looked up at the girls and Mrs. Bellaqua, who stared at him in fascination.

"I wonder what he's thinking," Robin said.

"I couldn't even begin to imagine, dearie," Mrs. Bellaqua said.

"I wish Vic would hurry," Jo said. "We never even found Mom."

"Ah, your poor mother," Mrs. Bellaqua said. "She was that tired. She came back looking like something the cat dragged in, so I told her to have a little toes up."

"A toes up?" Jo asked. "What's that?"

"A little nap, you'd say," Mrs. Bellaqua responded. "Well, here's your friend back now. Was your uncle there?"

"Yes. He'll be here in ten minutes," Vic said. "All we have to do is hang on till then."

CHAPTER TWELVE

The Mystery of Vic's Family

 It was a tense ten minutes. Robin's mouth ached from trying to smile reassuringly at the man. Finally, they heard the doorbell ring.

The man gestured at them. "No police," he growled.

"No police," said Mrs. Bellaqua. "Must go. Have to let Mr. Mountjoy in."

He let her leave the room, but motioned Robin, Jo, and Vic to stay where they were. Robin strained her ears. She heard footsteps on the landing.

Then she saw her mother's face.

"Robin, Jo, what's going on? What are you doing with that knife? Leave my girls alone!"

She tried to rush into the room, but Robin stopped her.

"He hasn't done anything yet, Mom. We're waiting for Vic's uncle to talk to him. He only speaks Japanese. Don't worry. It's going to be all right."

Mrs. Bridge ran her hand through her hair.

"Of course it's not all right. There's a strange man in your room and he's waving a knife around. I'll never forgive myself for letting you go out on your own. From now on, I'm keeping a close watch on you."

"No, Mom," cried Jo. "You can't do that to us."

Vic was trying to say everything would be all right, Jo was crying, and Robin was arguing with her mother while the Japanese man watched them, still holding his knife.

"Hello. What's going on?" Vic's uncle came into the room, walking carefully, Mrs. Bellaqua behind him.

Then he broke out into a big smile and bowed. The Japanese man bowed back.

"Ogawa-san," Uncle Peter said.

They began speaking rapid Japanese, the man waving his arms and pointing to the knives. Uncle Peter nodded his head and waved back at the girls and their mother.

"I think he's trying to explain who you are," Vic whispered to the girls.

More Japanese. More dramatic gestures. Finally, Uncle Peter burst out laughing and turned to the girls.

"Why did you take Mr. Ogawa's sushi knives?"

"His sushi knives. Who knew they were his sushi knives? We thought they were the Ripper's knives," Robin said.

"What made you think that?" Uncle Peter asked.

"The knives had six marks on them for the six people the Ripper killed," Robin said.

"Like these?" Uncle Peter pointed towards the six grooves carved in one of the knives.

"Yes. What else could they be?" Robin asked.

"They spell Mr. Ogawa's name in Japanese. That's how he writes his name, which means "small river" in English. These are his sushi knives. And this, ladies and gentleman, is my missing sushi chef."

He bowed to Mr. Ogawa, who bowed back.

"Your sushi chef?" Robin and Jo's mouths dropped open.

"Yes. I've been looking all over for him. And it appears he's been hiding out at your B&B all this time."

"Why was he hiding?"

"It seems he was too embarrassed to show up for his new job without his knives. You girls may not realize it but sushi knives are very, very valuable. He was very upset at losing them. He saw you take his case in the airport and tried to follow you, but he couldn't get into your train compartment. Then he tracked you to the B&B. He didn't know how to say what he wanted so he tried to get his case back by other means."

"You mean he tried to come into our room last night?" Jo asked.

The sushi chef hung his head when Uncle Peter translated.

"He's sorry he frightened you. He just wanted to get his knives back."

"And he followed us too, didn't he?" Robin asked.

"Yes, I'm afraid he did. He simply didn't know what to do or how to get his knives."

"But why didn't he call the police?" Robin asked.

"Mr. Mountjoy told us," their mother said. "Remember, he had a hard time with immigration. The poor man was terrified of anybody in uniform."

"Why didn't he just buy new knives?" Jo asked.

"These were made specially for him in Japan. To a sushi chef, his knives are part of him. If he lost them, it would be like losing an arm. Besides, they're very expensive to replace. He simply didn't have the money."

"I just can't get over the fact that you girls had these knives and never told me," wailed Mrs. Bridge.

"Mom, if we had told you, all you would have done was worried," said Robin.

"And it all turned out all right," said Jo.

"Promise me that if anything ever happens like this again, you'll tell me," said Mrs. Bridge.

"Of course," said Robin. She winked at Vic, but luckily Mrs. Bridge didn't see it.

"Honesty is always the best policy," Mrs. Bridge continued.

"Yes," said Uncle Peter, looking meaningfully at Vic, "it's always best to tell the truth."

Vic turned red and looked down at the floor. Mr. Ogawa said something to Uncle Peter.

"Mr. Ogawa wants to give you your case, Robin. He'll bring it up."

The sushi chef left the room, hugging his case to his chest.

Vic mumbled something to his uncle, but Robin couldn't hear. Jo glanced at her knowingly and smiled.

"I told you so," she mouthed.

Robin glared at her.

"Just ask them," Uncle Peter said to Vic.

Vic looked down at the floor again. Then he turned to Mrs. Bridge.

"My mother and father would like to meet you and the girls. Would you be able to come visit tomorrow?"

"That would be very nice," Mrs. Bridge said. "Are you sure it's no trouble?"

"No, they'd really like you to come," Vic said. "And of course, I'd like you to."

Mr. Ogawa came in and handed Robin her case. He bowed low and she bowed back.

"Thank you," she said.

"Now I'm taking my sushi chef back to the restaurant. Thank goodness that mystery is solved," said Uncle Peter.

"I'm sorry if we caused you any trouble," Robin said.

"Don't worry about it," Uncle Peter said. "It was really a clash of two cultures."

He turned to Jo. "You'll have that raw eel, yet, Jo. I'm sure Mr. Ogawa would be happy to make it for you."

Jo made a face and Uncle Peter laughed.

"I'll come by tomorrow at nine," Vic said, "and we'll take the train to my house together. It's about an hour out of London."

"Fine. We'll be ready, Vic," Robin said.

Then Vic left with his uncle and Mr. Ogawa.

"I declare, that was as good as a play or those dramas they have on the BBC," Mrs. Bellaqua said. "Who could imagine all that going on in my B&B? Well, all this isn't getting my work done, is it? I'll see you later, dearie," she said to Mrs. Bridge.

"I want to talk to you girls about something," Mrs. Bridge said sternly.

"Mom, we promise to be good," Jo said.

"I am sorry, Mom," Robin said.

"I did expect better from you, but that's not what I wanted to talk to you about. I just wanted to warn you to be polite tomorrow, no matter what Vic's house or parents are like."

"What do you mean?" Robin asked.

"You see, I told you there was something strange about him," Jo said. "Mom agrees with me."

"That's not what I meant," said Mrs. Bridge. "Vic is a perfectly nice boy."

Robin smiled and looked over at Jo.

"You see," she said, "there's nothing strange about him."

"But he may not have as much money as you do," Mrs. Bridge said. "He wears the same torn sweater all the time. And I get the feeling he's embarrassed about his house and his parents. They may be poor. It's up to all of us to make him feel comfortable, and for us to be polite and friendly."

"How could you think I wouldn't do that?" Robin said, angrily. "Vic's my friend. I wouldn't care if he lived in a pig sty."

"I would," said Jo, wrinkling her nose. "It might smell bad."

"Oh, you know what I mean," Robin said, stamping her foot. "You'd better be nice, Jo."

"I will be," Jo said. "Just don't tell me how to behave or what to think. I know there's something fishy about Vic, no matter what you say, Miss Robin."

"Fishy or not, stop it," said Mrs. Bridge. "He's a charming boy, and we'll all behave nicely tomorrow."

"I'm hungry," Jo said.

"I am too," Robin admitted. "Is it time for dinner, Mom?"

"Goodness, it's almost six o'clock. What a day! I'm glad your father will be back tomorrow night. Are you girls tired?"

"No, everything's been so exciting I'm not tired one bit," Robin said.

"Neither am I," Mrs. Bridge said. "How about you, Jo?"

"Oh, I'm a bouncy bean."

Jo bounced all the way to the Chinese restaurant Mrs. Bridge had chosen. After soup, dumplings, and chicken and beef, the girls were ready for a long walk. They ended up at the river, gazing at Big Ben and the Houses of Parliament.

"This is beautiful," Robin said. "This has been the best trip ever, Mom."

"Even with all that worry about the knives?"

"The best. We've seen and done so much. I loved it."

"It's not over yet. We have another week and a half to go," Mrs. Bridge said. "And the best part is Dad will be with us."

"Yay!" Jo said. "I can hardly wait." Then she yawned.

"Oh, dear," Mrs. Bridge said, gazing at the drooping Jo. "We still have to walk back to the B&B."

"You could carry me, Mom," Jo murmured.

"I think you're a little big for that," Mrs. Bridge said. "Everyone should have one cab ride in London. I think this is a good time for ours."

She hailed a big, black cab and they piled into it. Mrs. Bridge gave the address of the B&B.

"Do you know where that is?" she asked the driver.

"Oh, yes, madam. I know every address in London. You might not know this being a visitor here, but we London drivers have to study the city for a long time. Then we take a test. If we don't pass the test, we can't get our licenses."

As they barreled along the streets, Robin leaned back and dreamed about tomorrow. What would Vic's house look like? What would his parents be like? Her mother's warning came into her head and she imagined Vic living in a slum, his parents in ragged clothes.

The next day, Vic bundled them onto the train and made them sit by the windows.

"You'll be able to see the countryside this way."

At first, the train slid past grimy gray and yellow-brown houses stuck together with little patches of grass in the back. Then there were long stretches of empty fields. Robin began imagining Vic's home as a farm. Perhaps his father would be milking the cows, while his mother tended to the hens.

Soon the train was gliding past fields of hay with horses running in the distance. About ten minutes later, it came to a stop. The conductor mumbled a name and Vic said, "Here we are."

They climbed out of the train and onto the station platform. A man with a dark cap stood there waiting.

"There you are, sir," he said to Vic. "I hope you had a pleasant journey."

He led them to a long, dark car and opened the doors for them. Then he started the car and they drove off.

"Did you have to take a test to drive here?" Jo asked.

"No, Miss," the man said.

"Then it's not like London," she said.

"Not a bit, thank goodness. The air is clean and lovely here," the man said.

"I probably should tell you..." Vic said, miserably.

"Don't worry," Robin said.

The car swept up a long, graveled drive and stopped before a huge, old, brick house surrounded by flowers, trees, and shrubs. In the distance, Robin could see what looked like a park with a gazebo and trees and a stream.

"Is this where you live?" she asked, her mouth dropping open.

Before Vic could answer, a woman with blonde hair, dressed in a brown tweed suit, came down the front steps, followed by two brown and white dogs with floppy ears.

"Is this Mrs. Bridge, Vic?" she asked.

"Yes, Mother," Vic said.

His mother invited the Bridges inside, then looked at Vic.

"Oh, Vic, you're wearing that ragged sweater again. Can't you put something else on?"

"But it's comfortable," he protested.

She turned to the man who had driven them. "You can put the car away now, Briggs. We won't be needing it for a while."

"Yes, milady."

"Milady?" asked Mrs. Bridge.

"Yes, I'm Lady Cecily Mountjoy. My husband's Lord Richard. But please, just call me Cecily."

With a dazed expression on her face, Mrs. Bridge followed Lady Cecily into the house.

"I told you there was something fishy," muttered Jo, as she went in.

"Lord Richard! Lady Cecily! You never told me," Robin said to Vic.

"It's too embarrassing. Besides, I thought it might make a difference. I didn't want that to happen. People get so silly when they find out my parents have titles."

"Didn't you know I'd like you anyway, no matter what?"

"I hoped you would," Vic said.

"Of course."

As they walked up the steps, Robin thought of the difference between what she had expected and what had really happened, and she laughed.

Vic looked at her and said, "I guess this isn't where you thought I lived."

"You can't even imagine," said Robin. "Nothing's been what I expected about the Bridges in London, but it's all been great."

Robin Bridge's Glossary

While we were in London, I learned that although we speak the same language, the English call things by different names. Here are some examples:

American	English
ballpoint pen	biro
bathroom	loo, lavatory, toilet
cookie	biscuit
check (in a restaurant)	bill
dessert	pudding, sweet
elevator	lift
highway	motorway
Jell-O	jelly
mail	post
orchestra seats (in a theater)	stalls
pants	trousers
running shoes or sneakers	trainers
Santa Claus	Father Christmas
sidewalk	pavement
soccer	football
store	shop

American	English
subway	underground, tube
sweater	jumper, jersey
thanks	ta
tea	the drink, also a meal at 4 p.m. of sandwiches and cake
nap	toes up
truck	lorry

Cockney Slang

Uncle Peter gave us an introduction to Cockney slang when we had dinner at his restaurant. Very often, the second or rhyming part of the Cockney phrase is dropped, leaving the first word and making it even harder for outsiders to understand. For example, teeth might be "Hampsteads" or head would be "loaf."

Cockney	American
apples and pairs	stairs
butcher's hook (usually abbreviated as "give us a butch")	a look
dog and bone	phone
Hampstead Heath	teeth
jam jar	car
loaf of bread	head
plates of meat	feet
pork pies	eyes
Sweeney Todd	vice squad
Tom and Dick	sick
trouble and strife	wife

Robin Bridge's Guide to London

Remember, opening times and phone numbers change sometimes, so you'll probably want to call ahead when you plan to visit these places. If you're calling from the U.S., dial these numbers first before the number you want in London: 011-44-171. So if you wanted to call the British Museum from the U.S., you'd punch in 011-44-171-636-1555.

① The British Museum

This actually turned out to be a cool place. One day, while Mom was working, Jo and I spent half a day here. Here's what we saw. The Elgin Marbles—not so exciting looking but they do have an exciting history. Lord Elgin took them from Greece, now Greece wants them back. Room 17, the Assyrian reliefs, pictures of hunts carved in stone. You can actually see a king on his horse being attacked by lions. The mummies; not only are there people mummies, there are animal mummies, too—like a bull, an ape, a crocodile, a duck. In case you get hungry, there's a nice cafe selling sandwiches and teas on the ground floor.

Great Russell Street, WC1. ☎ 636-1555 (recorded information 580-1788). Monday–Saturday 10 a.m.–5 p.m., Sunday 2:30 p.m.–6 p.m. Admission free.

② Buckingham Palace, The Changing of the Guard

This is fun to see once, but not all that exciting. The Horse Guards are more fun because you can see them riding. The real Changing of the Guard is slow—about 40 minutes—so you're standing there staring at nothing for a long time. Still, Jo and I were glad we saw it. Don't get your hopes up about seeing the Queen. She never comes out at the Changing of the Guard except for special occasions.

Buckingham Palace, London, SW1. ☎ 123-411/505-452. Daily April–July, every other day August–March. 11:30 a.m.–12:10 p.m. Horse Guards: 11 a.m. weekdays, 10 a.m. Sunday.

③ Cabinet War Rooms

This was one of the best exhibits that Jo and I saw. These rooms were built deep below ground for Prime Minster Winston Churchill and his cabinet during World War II. From 1939 to 1945, Churchill ran the country from here. But he never slept here, even during the worst bombing. He found it too closed in and cramped. The exhibit has radio broadcasts to make you think you're back in those days. Someone told us that the place is exactly the way they left it in 1945. Wait till you see how tiny the bedrooms are!

Clive Steps, King Charles Street, London SW1. ☎ 930-6961. Daily 9:30 a.m.–5:15 p.m. Admission charged.

④ Chinatown

It's fun to walk through here and see the signs in Chinese and English. All the best Chinese restaurants are here. If you like dumplings, you can go here for lunch and have dim sum. Dim sum is most often steamed or fried dough filled with meat, chicken, or vegetables. There are also fried shrimp and fried chicken. Waiters and waitresses walk around the restaurant wheeling carts of food. You point to what you want to eat. Most of the dim sum are delicious. Even Jo liked them! But watch out for the chicken feet! If you walk down Newport Street, you will see a Japanese restaurant like the one Uncle Peter owns. It is called Tokyo Diner.

From the Leicester Square tube station, cross Shaftesbury Avenue and enter at Gerrard Street. The Chinese restaurants open early and stay open later than most others, till about 11 p.m.

⑤ Covent Garden

If you want to see jugglers, musicians, unicyclists, dancers, fire-eaters and puppet shows, this is the place to go. We could have stayed here for hours just watching people perform outside. For parents who get bored, there are plenty of shops inside the building. There are also lots of snack places in Covent Garden or nearby in case you get hungry.

Outdoor acts April–October all day.

⑥ Globe Theatre

Despite the fact that we fell asleep, the tour was pretty interesting. There's not much else to see yet. They weren't giving any performances when we went, and they were fixing up the exhibits, but there might be more when you go. One of the best things about the Globe is it's right near the water, with a great view of the other bank of the Thames.

New Globe Walk, Bankside, London SE1. ☎ 401-9919. Daily tours every half hour 10 a.m.–4 p.m. Admission charged.

⑦ The Guards Museum

The best part of this museum is the Toy Soldier Centre. Jo really loved it, and it was interesting to see all the different kinds of new and old miniature toy soldiers. Otherwise, there are too many uniforms in too many exhibits to look at. To get to the Toy Soldier Centre, go to the building on the right when you come in.

Wellington Barracks, Birdcage Walk, London, SW1. ☎ 414-3271. Daily 10 a.m.–4 p.m.

⑧ Hampton Court Palace

Not only is this a beautiful palace, but it's got a great maze. It was where Henry the Eighth (the one with all the wives) lived. First, you walk into the Great Hall. It's 60 feet high. We felt so small! Then there's the Great Kitchen with a fireplace large enough to hold seven wild boars or pigs. No wonder Henry was fat. The gardens are beautiful and there's even a tennis court. The most fun is the maze. It's made of bushes seven feet high, and, of course, Jo and I got lost. Someone told us later that if you take every right turn you can, you'll come out of the maze. There's much more to see, and we wanted to come back here but we didn't have time. Plan to spend the whole day.

Hampton Court, East Molesey, Surrey. ☎ 181-781-9500 (from the U.S., 011-44-181-781-9500). Open daily (mid-March–mid-October) 9:30 a.m.(10:15 Monday)–6 p.m.; daily (mid-October–mid-March) 9:30 a.m.–4 :30 p.m. Admission charged.

⑨ Hamley's

This is London's biggest toy store. What more can I say? Go here for all your toy needs. They have everything.

188-189 Regent Street, London, W1. ☎ 734-3161.

⑩ Harrods

Mom got carried away here and you'll see why. There are plenty of cheaper places to have tea, but the food looks so yummy, it's hard not to eat here. Go through the ground-floor food halls and look at all the candy and cookies. You won't believe it. It's like Halloween, Thanksgiving, and Christmas all rolled into one.

87-135 Brompton Road, Knightsbridge, SW1. ☎ 730-1234.

⑪ Houses of Parliament

This is where the British government does its business. It's like our Congress. It's a nice place to walk, particularly in the evening. The lights are on and the buildings are beautiful. We went on a tour one day, but it was pretty boring unless you're really into old buildings. Some politicians were talking but we didn't understand a word they said. It was more interesting to look at Big Ben, the enormous clock nearby, and to hear it strike the hour. Mom said that if the second light above Big Ben's face is lit, that means the people in Parliament are still in session. Sometimes they work until 1 a.m.

Parliament Square, London SW1. ☎ 219-4272. House of Commons open Monday and Thursday 2:30 p.m.–10 p.m., Friday 9:30 a.m.–3 p.m. House of Lords open Monday–Wednesday 2:30 p.m. on; Thursday 3:30 p.m. on.

⑫ Leicester Square

Leicester Square is the kind of place where there's always something going on. If you see a crowd gather, it's probably for a performance of the Swiss Centre's clock. Leicester Square has lots of fast food places for a snack (there's even a Häagen-Dazs ice cream parlor), and some big movie theaters that show Hollywood action films. There's not all that much else to see, but your parents might want to get half-price theater tickets here. There's a booth that sells them during the day.

⑬ London Zoo and Regent's Park

Do you know what an anoa is? A pudu? An okapi? Neither did we, but we saw them at this zoo. They have everything including the usual elephants, zebras, and tigers. During the day you can watch them feeding the animals. Jo and I were lucky enough to see them weighing the elephants and giving them a bath. There didn't seem to be any schedules for this, but most of the things happen between 12:30 p.m. and 3 p.m. Three things to remember: don't come on a rainy day because most of the animals are outside; get a map when you come because it's hard to figure out where everything is; also, forget what Jo said to Mom, you can feed the ducks!

Regent's Park, London NW1 4RY. ☎ 722-3333. Open daily 10 a.m.–5:30 p.m.; last admission at 4:30. Admission charged; family ticket available.

⑭ Madame Tussaud's

In spite of that little kid who scared me, I did have a good time here. But there were lots of wax figures of people I didn't know, mostly British people. The best part was the House of Horrors and the Spirit of London, a ride through history in a plastic black cab.

Marylebone Road, London NW1. ☎ 935-6861. Daily 10 a.m.–5:30 p.m. (opens 9:30 a.m. weekends and 9 a.m. during the summer). It's a good idea to call because they change their times a lot. Admission charged.

⑮ Museum of London

Jo and I really don't like museums. We've had to go to too many of them with Mom, but this one was different. We came back here twice because our admission ticket was good for three months! The things we liked the best were: (Robin) the woolly mammoth's tooth found near Downing Street where the Prime Minster lives; the Fire of London exhibit; and Cromwell's death mask (after he died, they put plaster of paris on his face and made a mask—really creepy if you think about it; (Jo) the Lord Mayor of London's coach (still used once a year on Lord Mayor's Day); the prison cell with 250-year-old graffiti; and the Ice Age exhibit.

150 London Wall, London EC2. ☎ 600-3699. Information 24 hours a day: 600-3699. Closed Monday, except bank holidays. Open

Tuesday–Sunday, 10 a.m.–5:50 p.m., Sunday, noon–5:30 p.m.
Admission charged.

⑯ Sherlock Holmes Museum

If you like Sherlock Holmes, like I do, you'll love this museum.
It's as if the great detective lived here, with an 1893 copy of the
newspaper, a gas fire, Doctor Watson's gun, and even Sherlock
Holmes's butterfly collection on display. The restaurant, Hudson's
Victorian Dining Room, was good and it was fun to try the food.

Museum: 221B Baker Street, London NW1 6XE. ☎ 935-8866.
Open daily 9:30 a.m.–6 p.m. Last admission is at 5:30 p.m.
Admission charged. Restaurant: 239 Baker Street, London NW1 6XE.
☎ 935-3130. Lunch noon–2:30 p.m., dinner 6 p.m.–10:30 p.m.

⑰ St. Paul's Cathedral

You can see the dome of this church from lots of places in London.
When you walk up to it, you see why. It's enormous. There are
lots of monuments to famous people here. But the thing that Jo
and I liked best was the Whispering Gallery. I stood with my face
close to the dome and Jo whispered from way across the other
side. I could hear her perfectly!

St. Paul's Churchyard, London EC4. ☎ 246-8348. Open daily
8:45 a.m.–4 p.m. (cathedral), 10 a.m.–4 p.m. (galleries and crypt).
Only adults have to pay.

⑱ Tower of London

This was my favorite place. First, you get to see where all the
prisoners were kept. The Beefeaters, those guys with the big,
black, bearskin hats, show you around. They tell you all the good
stuff about the beheadings and the tortures. Then you get to see
the Crown Jewels, which are amazing. They have the largest cut
diamond in the world. It weighs 530 carats. The average diamond
ring is about one carat or less—so you can just imagine. When

you walk outside, you're right near the Tower Bridge, the one everyone thinks of when they imagine a bridge in London.

If it's a nice day, the view is sensational. Also, I loved the Ceremony of the Keys in the evening—in spite of being scared.

Tower Hill, London EC3N 4AB. ☎ 709-0765. Open daily 9 a.m.– 6 p.m. March–October; 9 a.m.–5 p.m. November–February. Sunday, 10 a.m.–5 p.m. all year. The Jewel House might be closed for cleaning in January or February. Call before you go. Admission charged. Ceremony of the Keys: Tickets are free but only 70 people can go each night. Write for tickets way before you visit to the Resident Governor, The Queen's House, Tower of London, London EC3N 4AB.

⑲ Westminster Abbey

This and St. Paul's Cathedral are the churches everybody visits when they come to London. Westminster Abbey is one big cemetery. Almost everybody famous is buried here. It's more interesting to look at the throne in the center of the altar where the British kings and queens are crowned. Westminster Abbey is also where the funeral of Princess Diana was held. Jo and I liked the Abbey Museum, where they have a collection of royal death masks and wax figures. They've just put in a new life-size statue of Dr. Martin Luther King, Jr., here which Jo and I missed. That would be something to see.

Parliament Square, London SW1. ☎ 222-5152. Monday–Friday, 9 a.m.–4:45 p.m. (last admission at 4 p.m.); Saturday, 9 a.m.–2:45 p.m. (last admission at 2 p.m.) and 3:45 p.m.–5:45 p.m. (last admission at 5 p.m.). Open Sunday for services only. Admission charged.

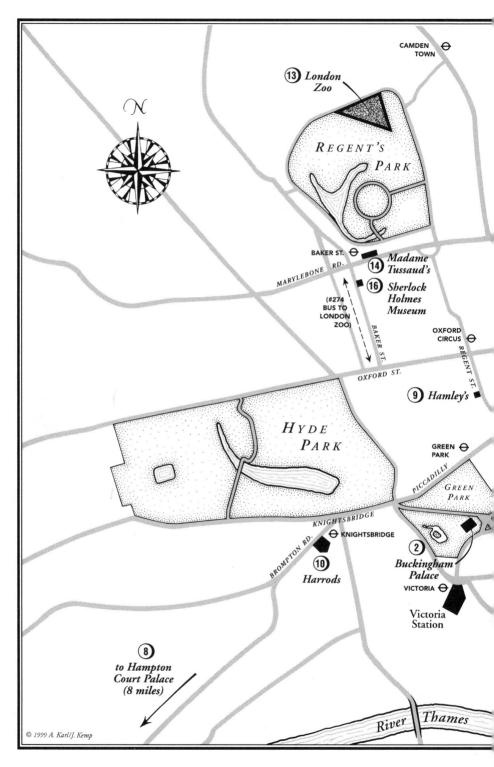